Sophia's War

Sophia's War
A Tale of the Revolution

BEACH LANE BOOKS
New York London Toronto Sydney New Delhi

BEACH LANE BOOKS

An imprint of Simon & Schuster Children's Publishing Division

1230 Avenue of the Americas, New York, New York 10020

This book is a work of fiction. Any references to historical events, real people, or real places are used fictitiously. Other names, characters, places, and events are products of the author's imagination, and any resemblance to actual events or places or persons, living or dead, is entirely coincidental.

Text copyright © 2012 by Avi Wortis, Inc.

Cover illustrations copyright © 2012 by Edel Rodriguez

All rights reserved, including the right of reproduction in whole or in part in any form.

BEACH LANE BOOKS is a trademark of Simon & Schuster, Inc.

For information about special discounts for bulk purchases, please contact Simon & Schuster Special Sales at 1-866-506-1949 or business@simonandschuster.com.

The Simon & Schuster Speakers Bureau can bring authors to your live event. For more information or to book an event, contact the Simon & Schuster Speakers Bureau at 1-866-248-3049 or visit our website at www.simonspeakers.com.

Also available in a Beach Lane Books hardcover edition

Book design by Debra Sfetsios-Conover

The text for this book is set in ITC Caslon 224 Std.

Manufactured in the United States of America

0813 OFF

First Beach Lane Books paperback edition September 2013

10 9 8 7 6 5 4 3 2 1

The Library of Congress has cataloged the hardcover edition as follows:

Library of Congress Cataloging-in-Publication Data

Avi, 1937–

Sophia's war : a tale of the Revolution / Avi.—1st ed.

p. cm.

Summary: In 1776, after witnessing the execution of Nathan Hale in New York City, newly occupied by the British army, young Sophia Calderwood resolves to do all she can to help the American cause, including becoming a spy.

ISBN 978-1-4424-1441-9 (hardcover)

ISBN 978-1-4424-1443-3 (eBook)

1. New York (N.Y.)—History—Revolution, 1775–1783—Juvenile fiction. [1. New York (N.Y.)—History—Revolution, 1775–1783—Fiction. 2. United States—History—Revolution, 1775–1783—Fiction. 3. United States—History—Revolution, 1775–1783—Prisoners and prisons—Fiction. 4. Spies—Fiction.] I. Title.

PZ7.A953Sq 2012

[Fic]—dc23

2012007962

ISBN 978-1-4424-1442-6 (pbk)

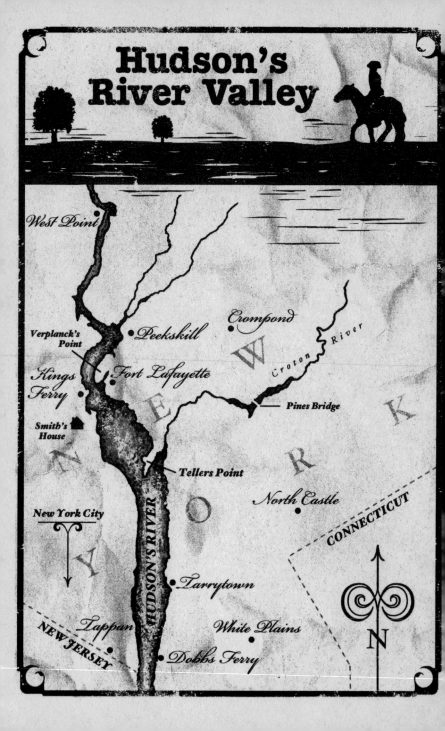

Hudson's River Valley

West Point

Verplanck's Point

Peekskill

Crompond

Croton River

Kings Ferry

Fort Lafayette

Pines Bridge

Smith's House

Tellers Point

New York City

North Castle

CONNECTICUT

NEW YORK

Tarrytown

HUDSON'S RIVER

Tappan

White Plains

NEW JERSEY

Dobbs Ferry

N

Contents

New York in 1776

Hudson's River

King's Wharf

King's College

BROADWAY

British Headquarters

Trinity Church

BROADWAY

Fort George

Sophia's Home

Sugarhouse

WALL STREET

Hanover Square

Peck's Slip

East River

SCALE OF FEET

0   400   1200   2000

Dear Reader:

It is a terrible thing to see a man hang. But that is why I did what I did. Was I right to act in such a way? You must decide. If, when you reach my last words, you cannot forgive me, so be it. Just know that although you will not find me in any history book, I shall tell the truth about what happened no matter how painful to me, the authoress of these words. For on these pages I have dared to put my trust in your heart.

Sophia Calderwood

PART ONE

1776

1

IN THE MOMENTOUS year of 1776, on the twenty-second of September, my mother and I were rushing back to the city of New York. New York was where I was born, and where I had lived peacefully until just a few weeks before, when we had fled in fear for our lives. The war for our country's independence had come to our door.

First, my brother, William, along with thousands of other patriot soldiers, ferried across the East River to the village of Brooklyn to defend the city from a British attack. Alarmed by the danger, my father warned us we might have to leave. And indeed, the Americans lost that battle and retreated through Manhattan as Great Britain gained complete control of the city.

But there was no news of William.

Desperately worried, I could only hope he was still with General Washington's army, and not taken prisoner. At times—though no one spoke it—we feared he had he been killed.

Too frightened to wait until we could find out, Father had said we must leave our house. It was a wise decision.

AVi ✦ 5

Soon after British troops occupied New York, a fire erupted and destroyed many buildings. But since we had taken flight to a friend's farm north of the city, we lacked information about our home's condition. Knowing that everything we had—money and possessions—might have been consumed in the fire, much of our lives was in awful derangement. After some days passed, Father and Mother decided that we must go home—if we still had one—and try to reclaim our lives.

Not sure how secure the way would be, Father made the decision that Mother and I, being females, should travel first. It was his belief that English soldiers would not harm a mother and child. "Are they not," he said, "our kinsmen and a civilized people?" Moreover, we would travel on a Sunday, Lords Day. Surely, all would be peaceful. As soon as Father determined that the roads were not dangerous for him, he would follow.

So it was that before dawn on Sunday morning, Mother and I, full of disquietude, set out to walk the twelve miles to the city. With me clutching Mother's hand tightly and barely looking up, we took the road called Harlem Lane. I may have been willowy for my twelve years of age, and my name *was* Sophia (the Greek word for "wisdom"), but you could just as well have called me "Frightened" and been done with it. In truth, as we hurried along, all my thoughts were on William. *He must come home!*

It was late morning when we reached the outskirts of New York. By then my wood-soled shoes were soaking wet, my ankle-length linsey-woolsey dress was mud spattered, and the laces of my bonnet—a mobcap—would not stay tied.

As we approached a ripe apple orchard, we observed a group of red-coated British soldiers, armed with muskets and bayonets, marching toward us. By their side, a drummer boy beat slow swinking strokes. An officer, a heavy, sweating man with a nose as bright red as his hair and uniform, strode along in high, black jack-boots. Following him was a Negro. His slave, I supposed.

In the middle of the soldiers was a man whose hands were tied behind his back. Looking to be in his mid-twenties, and some six feet in height, he was considerably taller than the soldiers who surrounded him. Dressed in civilian clothing, he wore no jacket and had a white muslin shirt open at the collar. His light brown hair was arranged pigtail-style. In the slanting morning light, I noticed his blue eyes. I will admit, I thought him handsome.

The young man walked with a dignified bearing, but his face was anything but serene. Rather, he bore a look of pale, raw intensity, with a gaze that appeared to be on nothing and everything at the same moment.

"What are they doing with that young man?" I said in a low voice to Mother.

She squeezed my hand, and in as fearful a voice as I had ever heard her utter, she said, "I think they are about to hang him."

Openmouthed, I watched as the men approached an apple tree upon which a ladder leaned. From a stout branch, a noose hung. Just beyond gaped an open grave, with a grave digger standing by, shovel in hand. We stopped and, along with a few other citizens, watched.

When the officer shoved the prisoner to the foot of the ladder, I heard the young man say, "May I have a . . . Bible?" His voice, low and steady, broke on the last word.

"No Bibles for damned rebel spies!" the officer shouted as if he wished us onlookers to hear. "Hoist him," he commanded.

Three redcoats, their faces blank, stepped forward. Two grabbed the young man's arms as if to restrain him, though I saw no attempt to break free. Would that he had! The third soldier placed the noose round the prisoner's neck and forced him up the ladder steps, even as another drew the rope tight under his chin.

As they did these things, each beat of the pulsing drum stabbed my heart.

Mother covered her lips with her fingers.

"Do you wish to confess?" the officer shouted.

I think the youth replied, but I was so appalled, I could not comprehend his words. In fact, such was my distress that I cried, "Have pity, sir. For God's sake!"

The officer glared at me. "Be still, missy, or you'll come to the same fate!"

I shrank behind Mother but peeked round to watch.

The officer turned back to his soldiers and shouted, "Swing the rebel off!"

One of the soldiers kicked the ladder away. The young man dropped. I gasped. His neck must have broken, for he died in an instant. Perhaps *that* was God's mercy.

Sometimes a hanging is nothing but slow strangulation.

Mother, pulling my hand, said, "Sophia! Come!" Sobbing, I stumbled away.

Later we learned that the young man's name was Nathan Hale. Over time, his death proved of greater consequence than his life. Without any doubt, it altered the history of my country as it altered mine. Indeed, what I had just witnessed was the beginning of my extraordinary adventures.

I shall tell you what happened.

2

FIRST, HOWEVER, YOU must know about my brother.

At seventeen years of age, William was five foot nine, with a lean face and bright eyes that seemed to want to observe everything. Such were his high spirits and boundless curiosity that Father referred to him—with a smile—as "our young fox."

The natural leader of many friends, William was determined to become a lawyer, a profession my parents encouraged. Once he even confided to me that his goal was nothing less than to become governor of the New York Colony. In short, he was the family heir, name, and hope. Our entire future. I was certain there was nothing he could not do.

Not only was William an early believer in our country's independence, he favored the abolition of slavery and thought women should be educated. Thus, it was William—not my parents—who took time to teach me my letters and how to write. Not only did I learn to read well and fast, he said my understanding and memory were excellent.

Whereas Mother believed such education would

diminish my chance of marriage, William proclaimed, "Only a man who can esteem Sophia's intelligence is worthy of her beauty."

What sister could not adore such a brother?

While William was an early follower of the radical Mr. Thomas Paine, Father was of a more traditional bent. They would debate for hours at a time, and enjoyed it. I tried to follow and, you may be sure, took William's side.

That said, the many swirling disputes and political events of 1776 were not fully understood by me. With patience, William tried to educate me. He talked, taught, and catechized me endlessly about our rights, freedoms, and natural liberties. He read me Mr. Paine's *Common Sense* in its entirety. Hardly a wonder that I considered my elder brother the source of all wisdom. Let it be said, that I, despite my age, could give an earnest defense of our rightful freedoms.

In September 1775, William began attending King's College. How proud I was to see him in his smart new black suit and cocked hat, with a volume of John Locke's *A Letter Concerning Toleration*, a gift from Father, tucked under his arm! He soon became friends with other young radicals, including Alexander Hamilton.

For some time, but especially during 1775 and into 1776, there had been turmoil in New York City. Disturbances and violent clashes erupted between those who supported the British monarchy (people labeled them "Tories" or "loyalists"), and those who, like my brother (and me), believed passionately that our liberties were being stolen by that "great brute" (Mr. Paine's words) King George III and his Parliament. The defenders of our rights—like William and his friends—called themselves "patriots." My own friends and I did no less.

The Boston Massacre, the battles of Lexington, Concord, and Bunker Hill, made the discord in New York more intense and brought on riots.

To the far north, Fort Ticonderoga was captured by the patriots Ethan Allen and Benedict Arnold. They removed the cannons and dragged them on sleds across New England, where they were used to liberate Boston.

Patriots everywhere rejoiced, none more so than I did.

Nonetheless, pro-British Tories remained in charge of the city. Red-coated British troops marched out of Fort George and tried to suppress what they called "the mob," the group that called itself the Sons of Liberty. William's college was closed. As a result, he became ever more active in politics and marched with the local militia.

As he paraded by, I stood near the road and cheered.

In the spring of 1776, patriot soldiers, led by General Charles Lee, came into town and simply took over. They forced the loyalists to give way.

Then George Washington and his Continental troops entered New York. When they arrived, many Tories—including the mayor—fled to safer havens along the Hudson Valley, to Long Island, Charleston, even to London.

William took me down to Bowling Green, by Fort George, and pointed out British ships of war, which lay anchored in the city's lower bay. "That's where many of the Tory cowards have fled," he told me. "Onto those ships."

Never mind that the ships bristled with guns.

But with the dispersal of the Tories, it was as though the plague had come to New York. The city became strangely vacant of citizens. Houses closed. Shops locked. As patriot soldiers prepared for the inevitable British attack, the town became a military camp. Many of our beautiful trees were chopped down so fortifications could be erected. Barricades were built. Few water vendors were to be seen on the streets. Merchant ships remained tied up at the wharfs, their sails furled like folded arms. Trade by land and sea—the true life of the town—all but ceased.

I was pleased to inform my anxious parents that "we" patriots could not fail to prevail.

Then in late June, an immense British fleet arrived and anchored in the Narrows, just off Staten Island. William took me to Fort George again, from where I saw a vast forest of masts.

He gazed at the formidable threat. "I promise you," he told me, "liberty shall always triumph over tyranny."

I had not a single doubt that he was right.

It was about then that he, at the urging of his good friend John Paulding, joined George Washington's army. So it was that just before that Brooklyn battle, William and John Paulding marched bravely away, muskets on their shoulders, sprigs of green in their hats in lieu of real uniforms. Sure that our soldiers, including my brother and his friend, would protect us, I cheered them off with pride.

Then, on August 22, in Brooklyn, more than fifteen thousand English and German troops attacked. Our soldiers were utterly defeated. Many were killed. As many as two thousand patriots were taken prisoner. Only a deft stratagem—and a thick fog—allowed General Washington to bring his reduced army back to Manhattan Island.

As one who could recite the crimes the British had committed—the ones cited in our Independence Declaration—I never considered that such a defeat could happen. Were not patriots in the right? Would not God Himself favor us? Was not our cause just? Was not my brave brother there?

When news of the defeat spread, as the patriot army fled through and away from the city, we patriots were greatly alarmed. I needed William to return. And his friend, too, Mr. Paulding.

We waited as long as it was deemed prudent. Then Father said we must find safety.

Shortly after we left, the fire erupted that destroyed a quarter of the town's buildings. The British claimed American rebels set it, and were on the lookout for arsonists and spies. Thus it came to be that Captain Nathan Hale—in regular life a schoolteacher in Connecticut—was taken.

Captured on Long Island, Hale was tricked into

revealing that he was a spy for General Washington. He was hauled into town, where the British Lord General Howe, head of the British Army, condemned him to be hung the next day. That, to my everlasting horror, is what we witnessed.

Dear Reader, I beg you, do *not* forget that Captain Hale was *hung* for being a spy. Over time, these consequences were enormous for me.

At that time, when American expectations were so badly bent, you may well understand my chief concern was William.

But I beg you not to misunderstand. I was still a passionate, if young, patriot.

3

AFTER WITNESSING CAPTAIN Hale's death, Mother and I, too numb to speak, continued into town. Passing Fresh Pond and then the Commons, we saw countless military tents. English soldiers, fully armed and in red uniforms, formed a sea of scarlet. German troops—many of whom bore fierce mustaches—were in their green uniforms. Scot troops were in their kilts.

We passed the new prison, called Bridewell. Though not fully built, men were being marched in. "Prisoners," Mother murmured. I prayed that William was still with General Washington.

On city streets, we saw that cobblestones had been pulled up. Barricades remained. As we reached Broadway, we began to grasp the great devastation wrought by the fire. Even beautiful Trinity Church was destroyed. Its gigantic steeple of 175 feet, its roof, and all within were gone, including a fine organ and library. The church building stood like part of its own forlorn cemetery.

Misery was everywhere. Tattered, soot-smudged citizens, reduced to beggary, poked though the wreckage of homes, searching midst scorched wood, blackened red bricks, and charred cedar roof shingles. The stench was awful.

Greatly agitated, Mother and I, holding our dresses up to avoid the mud, all but ran down Broadway. I gained some assurance when I saw that the east side of Broadway—our side—appeared for the most part intact, the spaced-apart houses unharmed. Nevertheless, gardens, usually so splendid in September, were choked with ash and weed.

Imagine our joy when we reached Wall Street and saw that our small, two-story wooden house was unscathed. Even better, the door was open. Perhaps William was home! We rushed inside.

Alas, no one was there. Moreover, much was in shambles, with some furniture destroyed, dishes smashed, and our four pewter plates gone. The old brass candlestick, a family heirloom of a hundred years, had disappeared from the mantel. As for the food we left in storage—nothing remained.

Mother went right to the hearth, stepped within, reached high, and pulled down the small iron chest Father had hidden. Opening it, she found our little hoard: twelve English sixpence, an English shilling, four crown pieces, plus two Spanish *reales*. Relief showed on Mother's face. Then I found an overlooked candle box. We would have some light.

But when we examined Father's workplace at the back of the house, we found much of it in disarray. Father was a scrivener, a copier of legal documents as well as a copy editor for the newspaper publishers, both Mr. Rivington (publisher of the *Gazette*) and Mr. Gaine (publisher of the *Mercury*). Many of Father's treasured books—his Johnson dictionary, his Pope, Locke, Richardson, his adored *Robinson Crusoe*—lay torn and broken. Spilled ink made frozen shadows on the floor. Quills lay scattered like a bird ripped apart.

Mother latched the front door and said, "At least we have our home and savings."

"And William," I insisted.

Though I knew Mother was in great anxiety about him too, all she said was "We can only pray for good news." Then, after a painful sigh—a better reflection of her feelings—she said, "We'd best try to put things in order."

I found some ease in doing something useful.

We were still cleaning when a harsh pounding came upon our door. Hoping it was one of our neighbors, I hastened to open it. Standing before the house was a troop of five British soldiers, all armed.

4

IN FRONT OF the soldiers stood an officer in a red regimental jacket complete with gold facings. He had a lengthy nose, a jutting chin, and a severe frown. A sword was at his side.

"Sophia," Mother called. "Who is it?"

When I could find no words to reply, Mother came up behind me and looked. When she did, she gasped.

The officer made a curt bow. "Good afternoon, madam," he said in a Scot's accent. "Captain Mackenzie. Is your husband at home?"

"He's—We expect Mr. Calderwood soon, sir," said Mother.

"Where is he?" he snapped.

"I'm not sure, sir," Mother replied. "He's been hiding from the rebel army."

Her words took me by surprise. I had never known Mother to lie.

"There's nothing from which to hide, madam," said the officer. "They have been roundly defeated. Your husband's name?"

"Hiram Calderwood."

Captain Mackenzie made a gesture. One of the soldiers, a sheaf of papers in hand, came forward and sorted through his lists. "He's here, sir," he announced.

Captain Mackenzie nodded and said, "Good." To my mother he said, "What's your husband's trade?"

"A scrivener, sir. He most often works for Mr. Rivington and Mr. Gaine."

"I know naught of them."

"They publish loyalist newspapers."

"I'm pleased to hear it," said Captain Mackenzie dryly. Next moment he issued an order to his men: "Search the house."

The redcoats acted as if we were not there. They opened cupboards, poked about the hearth—thank goodness we had retrieved the money—and went upstairs, where they searched under my parents' bed, hauled out my trundle bed, and even broke open a trunk from which they dragged winter blankets. All was strewn about. Loathing them with all my heart, I renewed my rebellious vows.

Their most intense search was in Father's office. Papers and books were scrutinized. At one point, a soldier approached the captain with a pamphlet in his hand.

Captain Mackenzie read the title aloud. "*Common Sense*," he announced. "Do you know what this is, madam?"

"No, sir," said Mother. Another falsehood!

"An incitement to rebellion," said the captain. "I presume your husband read this. Does he credit what it says?"

"I'm sure Mr. Calderwood doesn't, sir," said my mother.

I know otherwise, I thought with pride.

Grimacing, Captain Mackenzie ripped the pamphlet and tossed the pieces away. To my mother, he said, "Madam, if your husband does not return soon, he'll be accounted a rebel and shall lose this house. If he does come back, he must subscribe his allegiance to the king at Scots Tavern, near City Hall. I warmly advise, madam, he wear the red ribbon to identify himself as a loyal subject." He made a motion. One of the soldiers opened a pouch and held out a strip of red cloth.

Mother bobbed a curtsy and took it. "I'll be sure to tell him, sir."

"Finally," the officer went on, "that room, where I presume your husband conducts his business, must be converted into your own sleeping quarters. The upstairs room will be taken over by the army."

"Sir?"

"My orders are to find accommodations for our officers. You'll be paid rent for the officer's billeting."

"When will your officer arrive?"

"Soon. Be so kind as to have the upstairs rooms in order. Good day to you, madam!"

Captain Mackenzie made a curt bow and ordered his soldiers to depart.

I shut the door behind them. Furious, I turned to Mother. "What were they looking for?"

"Evidence that your father was a rebel."

I declared, "Father cannot sign that oath."

Mother, fingering the red ribbon, said, "Sophia, Mr. Calderwood will sign that oath if we wish to remain here."

"But if he doesn't believe—"

"Child!" snapped Mother. "What we think and what we say can no longer be the same! And we must not mention William."

I took refuge in the fact that she called me "child" only when distraught.

"What if he appears?"

She glared at me. "Did you not see that hanging?"

That silenced me, for a moment. Then I said, "When do you think that British officer—the one who will stay here—will come?"

"The officer said 'soon,'" Mother answered. "Let's trust that Mr. Calderwood comes first, and unharmed. But you heard the officer. If your father doesn't arrive, we'll lose this house."

"He will come, won't he?"

"I pray."

"We need William here."

"Sophia," my mother said in her most severe voice, "find your own courage!"

I was too dismayed to speak.

"Let's get back to work," said Mother, and she began by gathering up the torn pages of *Common Sense* and tossing them into the hearth.

In haste, I set to. All the while, I wondered what it would be like to have a stranger in our home. A British officer at that! I kept thinking of the officer who led

Captain Hale to his death. What if *he* came to live with us. Or another as brutal? I supposed all were alike. Whoever he was, I knew I should despise him. But how would I ever learn to keep my emotions bottled? I was an ardent patriot. If I could not keep it secret, I knew the consequence.

Then I reminded myself: it didn't matter what I felt. Regardless, there was a fair likelihood we might yet lose our home, and worse.

5

AFTER WE HAD worked, cleaning and scrubbing and putting such furniture as remained back in place, Mother stood in the center of the almost empty common room. Her face was tense, her eyes closed. I could see her suffering.

"I'm sorry," she said, "to have been cross. It's difficult to know what to say or do."

"Could we send a message to Father that he needs to hurry?"

"Impossible."

"Is there any place we could search for William?"

"I don't know where except that new prison."

"Then we should go," I urged.

Mother found a pin and attached the red ribbon to her sleeve. "Hopefully," she said, "this will protect us."

Latching the door, we set out along Broadway toward the Commons, some eight or nine streets north. The nearer we approached, the more British troops we saw.

I have learned that heart and eyes are one. That's to say, one can *see* a thing, but when one is *linked* to it, the seeing is different. I had observed the new prison before. This time, as I drew closer, aware that my brother could be a prisoner, I now grasped how formidable a fortress it was.

It had two stories of brick, some fifteen windows across—all with visible bars. The center section was three stories high. Chimneys stood at either end, plus four in the middle. Before the entryway stood a troop of redcoats on guard. A fence was all about.

We stood and studied it. "Come," Mother said at last. We moved toward the entryway and stopped in front of the soldiers.

"Please, sir," Mother said to an officer who seemed to be in charge. "Can I find out if my son is in the prison?"

"A rebel?"

"He joined General Washington's army."

"You can apply for information at the City Hall."

"But—"

"Move on, madam!"

We retreated.

Struggling not to cry, I waited for Mother to decide what next to do. At length she said, "We'd best find some food."

Turning south and east, not talking, me gripping her arm, we went along narrow Maiden Lane toward the Fly Market, where we usually did our marketing. The market was by the East River docks, near the Long Island ferry.

When we met a few friends, news was exchanged in hushed and uneasy tones. Mother spoke of the hanging we had witnessed. That's how we learned the young man's name. In addition, we were told how the American soldiers, having retreated through Manhattan, had continued their withdrawal. Though almost cut off by the English, most (so we were informed) happily reached security. The American troops did strike back with some small success, but our forces were obliged to retreat farther. The only patriot soldiers remaining on Manhattan Island were at the far north end, in Fort Washington. Whereas New York's population had been some twenty thousand, hardly more than five thousand civilians remained.

"We are at the mercy of the British," a friend of my mother's confided. Another said, "It's the end of patriot dreams."

Though I refused to believe that, it was not for me, a girl, to dispute such thoughts.

When we reached the Fly Market, it was startling to see what had happened. Beneath the long, open shed, many stalls had been abandoned or destroyed. Remaining vendors had little to offer. The shortages were because the ferries, which normally brought food from Long Island and Jersey, had been curtailed. Accordingly, costs were shockingly high. We were lucky to get an old cabbage, a three-pound loaf of stale bread, and some Indian corn for fourteen pence.

We hurried home. When we got there, I was relieved that the British officer had not arrived. However, neither had Father. Or William.

After I drew water from the street pump on Broadway,

Mother cooked the cabbage in the hearth, using the one pot that had not been stolen. For firewood, we used pieces of broken chairs. To light the fire I had to go two houses down, to Mr. Porteus's house, and beg a glowing ember from a frightened servant. The fire lit, the pages of *Common Sense* withered like dead flowers.

By the time we had eaten and tidied as best we could, it was dark. Our inside shutters were closed. Father still had not returned. No word of William.

As Mother and I sat in the tense and murky stillness, I heard the tramp of feet on the street. I leaped up, cracked open a shutter, and peeked out. A troop of British soldiers was marching down the way. As they passed, I heard the shouted command: "All citizens shall remain in their homes during curfew on pain of severe punishment!" It was repeated, ever fainter, as the crier passed along.

I crept back to Mother. The same fears I had before—about Father, William, the war—filled my mind and heart. Both were heavy. We did not speak, just held hands.

In time, she said, "Best to bed."

As she banked the fire, I latched the front door. We bedded in my parents' room, on the second floor. As we lay down—fully clothed—I was aware that we were sleeping there for the last time. I slept by her side, not in the low trundle where I usually reposed.

I could not rest. My worrying was too intense. I kept trying to rid myself, too, of images of that hanging.

Oh, the pity I felt for that young man. The cruelty! I could not deny the fear and hatred I had of the British soldiers.

Which comes first, I asked myself, fear or hatred?

By the moonlight that seeped through our one small window, I wondered what trials would be ours on the morrow. Accordingly, I prayed hard, not only for Father's and for William's safety, but that our cause would not falter, and that I might find courage for myself. Though not sure it would be bestowed, I knew I would need it.

Indeed, I did need it and very soon.

6

DAYLIGHT CAME AFTER but a poor night's sleep. I worked first with Mother cleaning the upstairs room, and then we turned Father's office into a bedroom for the three of us. It was good to be busy, for it distracted me from dismal thoughts of Father and William. Yet as hours passed, with no word from either, my concerns only multiplied.

Mother gave permission for me to go to the nearby homes of two dear friends, Pamela Jones and Constance Wright. I found their houses boarded, doors marked "GR," or "George Rex." Such a mark meant the British Army considered the occupants rebels and that they were taking possession of the house. I had no idea where my friends were. Indeed, I never saw them again.

When night came, I told myself that Father and William would—must—be home next day. At least the house was in readiness.

That night, as we went to bed in the new room, I listened to the watch going by: "All citizens shall remain in their homes during curfew on pain of severe punishment!"

Huddled beneath the blanket, I began to wish Father would *not* come until the morning. After a while, there were no further sounds, not even the normal tread of the city's black slaves carrying night soil to the river. With that thought, I drifted into sleep.

In the middle of the night, a sound woke me. I sat up but saw nothing save a blade of pale golden moonlight sliding through a gap in the window shutter. Uncertain if I had really heard anything, I listened hard. A creaking; perhaps a swinging sign. The bang of what I hoped was a shutter. The soft moan of wind, which my brainwork told me was the despondent soul of Captain Hale. Perhaps he knew of my pity and had come in search of comfort.

Shivering, I sank beneath the blanket and edged closer to Mother, only to hear the noise come again. That time I was sure it was tapping. When it came yet again, I became convinced it was upon our front door.

"Mother—"

She stirred. "What?"

"I think someone's at our door."

She pushed herself up. We both listened. The tapping came again.

I squeezed her arm, "Do you think it's that officer? Are they about to take our house?"

"Stay," she said, then slipped out of bed, wrapped her robe about, and went into the common room. I crept after her and watched as she pressed against the door. "Who is it?" she called.

"It's me!" I heard.

Father's voice!

Mother pulled the door open, and there was Father. My heart rejoiced! But then he staggered forward, and in the feeble light, I saw how gaunt and ill he appeared. His clothing was torn and, in places, blood spattered.

In haste, Mother shut and latched the door behind him. Swinging about, she tried to embrace him. He winced and moved away, panting so, he could not speak. He was holding his right arm in an awkward position.

"Mr. Calderwood!" cried Mother. "What's happened?"

"As I was . . . coming through . . . the lines," he stammered, "I was shot. Struck in the arm. But I am overjoyed to see you, Miss Saville." Molly Saville was Mother's maiden name, and Father would, in moments of affection, call her "Miss Saville."

Mother guided him to the settle. Using an ember from the hearth, she lit a candle. Wide-eyed, I stood by as she stripped off his torn and bloody shirt. He recoiled in pain. When I saw a jagged wound in the upper part of his right arm, I shrank back.

He said, "Any news of William?"

When Mother said, "Nothing," he closed his eyes.

"Fetch some water!" Mother called to me.

I grabbed pot and candle, and, heedless of the night watch, dashed out to the street pump. When I got back, the fire was ablaze. As Mother heated the water, Father told us haltingly what had happened to him.

Word had come to the farm where we'd been that British troops were scouring the countryside, arresting *all* men, rebel or no. Fearful of what might happen if soldiers arrived at the farm, and not wishing to make difficulties for his friends, he started for home as soon as night descended. Somewhere north of town, he came upon a British patrol. Not stopping lest he be taken prisoner, he bolted. That's when he was shot.

"I don't think the ball struck bone," he said in a low, strained voice. Each passing moment he seemed to weaken.

Mother turned to me. "Sophia, you need to get Dr. Dastuge." The doctor lived farther down along Broadway.

Even as I heard my mother speak, I, recollecting the crier's call, "All citizens shall remain in their homes on pain of severe punishment," was too fearful to move.

"Sophia, it's urgent! You just went for water. And it will be dawn soon. You must go now. No, wait!"

She hurried to where we had been sleeping. When she returned, the red ribbon was in her hand. After placing my cape about my shoulders, she pinned the red ribbon to the collar.

"Shall I take the candle?"

"It will only draw attention. Now quickly!" she said. "And be watchful." Opening the door, she all but shoved me out.

⁍ 7 ⁌

THE LATCH CLICKED behind me. Waiting for my heart to settle, I stood on the stone step and gazed about. Not so much as a needle of light escaped from the house. To the east, a little light—a band of Dutch orange—lay low, a promise of a fair day. In the air, a tang of salt sea, along with a whiff of charred wood. From somewhere overhead, a squawking seagull.

Though most city streets were narrow and crooked, Broadway was wide and straight, so I was able to glance up and down. Not a soul. I reminded myself where I had to go, a few streets in a southerly direction. Normally an easy walk. At that moment it seemed very far.

Shivering with cold fear, I strengthened my will by reminding myself of Father's need. But as I set off, my heartbeat, my panting breath, my footsteps on cobblestones, seemed as loud as thunderstorms. Nay, louder. But then, all noise alarms when it is surrounded by a fearsome silence.

I pressed on, only to spy some people standing close together in the street. Frightened, I stopped and gawked. It was three tall men, theirs faces ghostlike.

One of them lifted a lantern. With the light bright in my eyes, I forced myself forward. Drawing closer, I saw they were three British soldiers, red jacketed, with white trousers and black boots. Their tall, fur hats— what they called busbies—towered over me. In their hands were muskets with bayonets. One of those guns was pointed right at me.

"Halt!"

Panic-struck, I decided that boldness might be perceived as innocence. I went on, my breathing quick, my steps hesitant, my heart a hammer.

"Why are you on the street?" demanded an angry voice. "There's a curfew."

I swallowed hard, then said, "Please, sir, I'm fetching Dr. Dastuge. For my father. He has a fever."

The one who held the lantern lifted it higher, as if to appraise me. Perhaps he saw the red ribbon on my cape.

"Your name?" he demanded.

"Sophia," I said, and then added with a stroke of daring, "the same as the king's daughter."

The lantern lowered. One of the soldiers said, "Where does this doctor reside?" His voice was softer.

"Broadway. Number 276, I think. Just one street further."

"We'll guide you."

"Thank you, sir."

Wanting no second invitation, I darted forward and skirted the soldiers, not wishing to even glance at them. They came right behind.

"Are you thankful we drove the rebels out?" one of the soldiers asked from behind my back.

"Of course, sir," I replied, afraid to look round lest they see the lie upon my face.

"We're only here to restore the king's peace," another of them said.

"I'm pleased," I said, but to myself, I thought, *Is this what our lives will be like, constantly lying?*

In moments, I was before the doctor's home. I glanced back at the soldiers to ask permission. When one nodded, I knocked.

It was some time before the door opened a wedge. "Yes?"

It was Dr. Dastuge himself. Had his family and servants fled? He was a short, stout man, bald, with a fat and grizzled face. When he drew close and wheezed, I smelled liquor.

In a low voice, so the soldiers would not hear, I told him of Father's injury.

"A bullet?" he rewhispered.

"Yes, sir," I replied. "I told the soldiers escorting me that it was a fever."

He rubbed his bulging, red-rimmed eyes with a fat and dirty finger, hoisted a small wooden chest, and gave me a nod. "Lead the way."

I returned along Broadway, the doctor at my side, his gait clumsy, his breath a periodic *puff*. Daylight increased. A rooster crowed from somewhere. The soldiers remained close. But the nearer we came to my house, the more I feared that the soldiers would enter and discover Father's true condition. Knowing that captured rebels were being put in prisons, I made a desperate, silent prayer: *Do not come in.*

⋆ 8 ⋆

UPON REACHING OUR door, I turned toward the soldiers. "Thank you, sirs," I said.

One touched a finger to his busby. "Happy to be helpful, miss," he said. And they went off. Allowing myself a breath, I watched them go. I had to admit that they had been kind.

The doctor entered our dim house. I followed, shutting the door behind me.

"Good morning to you, madam," said the doctor.

"Thank you for coming," Mother returned in a hushed voice, her eyes bright with tears. "Mr. Calderwood is in the back room. Did my daughter tell you—"

"She did, madam. A lodged musket ball." He held up his box. "My instruments. Bring a candle."

Mother said, "Sophia, stay here."

She led the doctor away, while I sat before the hearth. The low, flickering flames caused shadows to gambol all about me. Trembling, I drew my cloak tight. From the back room, I began to hear muffled voices. First Mother's, then Father's—(faintly), then, finally, the doctor's. I strained to listen. When Father moaned, I pressed my hands together so tightly they ached.

Quiet resumed. All I could do was wait. *William still missing. Father wounded. Mother in tears. Before my eyes, the image of that hanging.* I began to shiver uncontrollably. "Sophia," I scolded myself. "Be brave. Be brave!" I whispered the Lord's Prayer. I said the first few sentences of our Declaration, which William had insisted I learn: "We hold these truths . . ." *Be strong*, I told myself over and over again.

The back room door opened. The doctor emerged looking more disheveled than before. Bloodstains soiled his shirt.

Mother, looking wan, followed.

"Keep him abed," the doctor advised her. "I shall look in later. I wish you a good day, madam."

"The like to you," she said.

I hurried to open the door.

The doctor gave me a nod and left. I shut the door and turned to Mother. She was holding her hands to her eyes.

I said, "Is he is all right?"

"He should be." She held out her hand. In her palm lay a musket ball. It was bloody. "He'll need time to heal. I don't know what use of his arm or hand he'll have."

I peeked into the back room. Father lay abed. Eyes closed, hands resting on the bloodstained coverlet, he appeared to sleep. I retreated.

In the common room, Mother was sitting in the chair, slumped over.

"Can I do anything?" I said.

"You fetched the doctor."

"Soldiers stopped me along the way."

"What did you say?"

"I lied."

Her glance showed approval. "It is hard."

I said, "At least we'll not lose the house."

"The British officer has yet to come," she said.

We sat side by side, not speaking. At length Mother stood up. "We can't sit like this." She raked up the fire and set Indian corn to boil in the pot.

"Sometime this morning," she told me, "you must see if Mr. Gaine or Mr. Rivington are about."

As I have explained, Father worked for these newspaper printers. I had been to their shops with Father many times and had taken messages back and forth, so I knew his employers fairly well, as they knew me.

Mother said, "You'll tell them he's in the city."

"Can he work?"

"He needs the pay. Since the work is usually done here, you can help him. I'm glad William taught you to read."

I nodded.

Mother was silent a while. Then she said, "Things are so topsy-turvy, I'm not sure the printers will even be here."

"Shall I tell them what happened to him?"

"I don't know what side they are on."

I thought for a moment and then said, "Mother, who am I to trust?"

She considered my question. "Me. Father." And then she said, "And William—if he returns."

The word "if" rang as loudly as a fire bell.

✲ 9 ✲

MIDMORNING, THE DAY cool and bright, I set out to see the printers. Many soldiers were on the streets. Missing were traders, mechanics, vendors, and clergy. And mind, the city had more than two hundred churches. Children were scarce. Citizens were dazed and wary and appeared to keep their distance one from another.

What a contrast to the British soldiers. They strode about like the loud, boisterous victors they were, devils of fear and disorder. They repeatedly made ill-mannered remarks to civilians, to women more than men. Hoping to avoid their indelicacy, I worked to look the other way.

I went first to Mr. Rivington's shop at the other end of Wall Street, where he had his press. He also sold books and medicines, like Bateman's Golden Spirit of Scurvy Grass, which Mother once made me take, and Dr. Ryan's Incomparable Worm-Destroying Sugar Plumbs, which, thankfully, she did not. The place was closed, but a man who was loitering about told me Mr. Rivington was yet in London, where he had fled from the Sons of Liberty some time ago.

I walked on to Hanover Square, in the southern part

of town, the wealthy ward. Though called a square, it was in fact, triangular. Right off Queen Street, it had fine houses, both wood and brick, along with shops, business establishments, and taverns. Fortunately, it was untouched by the fire.

Mr. Gaine had a three-story building, with a sign depicting a Bible and a crown, his mark. He and his family lived above, while the lower floor was where he had his press, which produced his newspaper, the *Mercury*.

I walked in. The smell of printer's ink, a mix of varnish and lampblack, filled the air. Mr. Gaine published books and sold goods ranging from dice boxes and paper to reading glasses, lead pencils, medicines, plus many small items of general utility. One wall bore samples of the blank legal forms that he also printed: mortgages, deeds, invoices, and the like. Another wall had upper and lower cases of type—with many small compartments. From ceiling rafters, sheets of damp paper hung in readiness for printing.

The room was centered by the large wooden press with its stone form for holding the type, the crank that rolled the paper forward, and the screw and lever, which pressed type to paper.

On the floor was a boy on his hands and knees.

As I watched, he picked up some bits and put them in a small leathern bucket that was by his side. His fingertips were black. When he paid no mind to me, I finally said, "Good day."

The boy took note of me, sat back on his legs, and touched a finger to his forehead, leaving a black mark.

"James Penny," he informed me. I took him to be about ten years of age, with a round, smudged face and curly brown hair. He wore no shoes.

"Is Mr. Gaine here?" I asked.

"No."

"Where is he?"

"Over to Jersey."

"Has he fled?"

The boy studied me before answering, as if trying to decide what to say. The thought came: *No one knows whom to trust.* When he spoke, it was only to say, "I suppose he'll be back."

"When?"

"Soon, maybe. Not sure. Who are you? What do you want?"

"My father is Mr. Calderwood. He does copy work for Mr. Gaine."

"The *Mercury* is being published by Mr. Serle these days. Lord Howe's man."

I said, "My father sends his respects and says he's prepared to work for your master again."

"Want me to tell Mr. Serle?"

"If you'd be so kind."

"And if Mr. Gaine gets back, I'll tell him."

The "if" word again.

"Good day," the servant boy murmured, and turned back to the floor.

I said, "What are you doing?"

"Picking up type. Got all dumped. Always happening."

"Good day," I said again, and retreated.

Not sure what my parents would make of the disappointing news about Mr. Gaine and Mr. Rivington, I set off for home, going along Willard Street.

I had not gone far when I heard the tramp of feet. Turning, I saw, hedged in by armed British soldiers, a parade of ragged men. A fair number had bandages wrapped about heads or arms, some of which bore brown stains of old blood. To a man, they had disconsolate looks and did not walk so much as shuffle. I recognized a few as citizens of the town who had been active among the radicals. One I think was William's friend.

In front of this procession marched the same portly, red-haired officer I had seen leading Captain Hale to his death. Just to see him made me fear that these prisoners were to suffer the same fate as Captain Hale.

Though I searched for my brother among the men, he was not to be found. I did wonder if anyone had news of him but was sure I'd not be allowed to exchange words.

I turned to a gentleman who, like me, had paused to watch.

"Where are they being taken?" I said.

"Off to the new jail, the Bridewell, I suspect. That's the provost, Cunningham, in the lead."

I glanced about nervously. "What will happen to them?"

"The prisoners? No notion," said the man, without much sympathy, I thought.

My heart heavy, I watched the wretched men go by. Behind them, I saw two additional British officers. In utter contrast to the prisoners, they were dressed with care, in scarlet coats with blue facings, sash and sword. They wore high busbies. The two were talking to each other with animation and laughing.

As I looked on, I noticed a prisoner who struggled somewhat behind the others. One of the officers also saw him. He drew his sword—which made me recoil—and with the flat of it, struck the man on his backside, shouting, "Move on, rebel!"

Even as he hit the defenseless prisoner, he laughed. I detested him with all my heart.

When the prisoners continued to march northward, the young officer did not follow. Instead, he glanced at a piece of paper he had in hand, saluted his fellow officer, then turned west down Maiden Lane.

Though it vexed me greatly that this cruel fellow was going in the same direction I must go, there was nothing for it but to follow. Not wishing to be near, I kept back and waited for him to turn off in some other direction.

Alas, he continued to walk the same way as I, going straight until he reached Broadway. There he paused, consulted his paper, and moved toward our house. When I saw him knock upon *our* door, it came to me like summer thunder: this cruel British soldier must be our boarder.

10

MOTHER OPENED THE DOOR.

The officer touched his hat in a salute and made a slight bow. "Madam," I heard him say in a bright, cheerful fashion, "your most humble servant. Lieutenant John André, Seventh Foot, Royal Fusiliers."

Mother stared at him in astonishment. She said, "How can I help you, sir?"

The lieutenant held out his paper. "It's my pleasant duty to inform you, madam, that I have been ordered by Commandant Robertson to reside here. While I have no doubt it may be somewhat inconvenient, such are the fortunes of war. I assure you, madam, it's my desire that you will find me courteous, appreciative, and no burden to your generous hospitality."

It was not a speech I expected.

Mother, clearly uncertain what to do or say, stood gawking at the soldier. Then she noticed me standing on the street, looking on. "Sophia," she called. "Come. Our boarder has arrived."

The officer turned and I truly saw him. He was a youngish man of middling height, olive complexioned, with black hair and a cheerful, graceful air. Upon seeing me, he offered a bright smile, which I had to admit was frank and open.

To my mother he said, "Is this your daughter?"

"Yes, sir, she is."

"Your servant," he said to me, with a bit of a dip. In all my life, I had never been bowed to before, much less heard such polite address as "Your servant." Besides, I thought myself a girl, not a lady. That said, I was flattered. Indeed, his cheerful civility put me into confusion, from which I was saved when Mother said to him, "Please come in, sir."

Even then the soldier paused, turned toward me, and with a polite gesture, indicated that he wished *me* to enter first. His condescension was a further bewilderment to me, who had resolved to hate the man. Yet I could hardly remain upon the street. Instead, in what I thought was a haughty, frosty manner (childishly contrived), I walked past him and into the house.

He took off his tall hat and followed.

The three of us stood in the common room in momentary awkwardness. The lieutenant gazed at the sparseness and spoke to my mother, with an occasional glance at me. "Madam, I thank you for your welcome," he said as if he had been an invited guest. "My primary regret is that it's this war, this unnatural rebellion—like some brother-to-brother squabble—which brings us together.

"My deepest desire is that our small differences will soon be peacefully resolved to the benefit of all. In the meanwhile, I am sure we can make the best of it. I am not one to rise at a feather. And when I tell you that I have only lately come from the wilds of Pennsylvania, where I was held a prisoner by a greasy committee of dullards, you may believe I'm heartily delighted to be here."

The kind speech flustered my thoughts.

"Thank you, sir," Mother said. "Shall we show you your room?"

"You are most kind."

Mother turned to me. "Sophia, be so good . . ."

That she had asked me to do the honors took me by surprise, until I grasped that she needed to inform Father who had come, so as to decide what to reveal to the officer about his condition.

It was I, then, who led John André to our upstairs room. Once there he gazed about. "This will be fine," he said. "And a trundle bed! Perfect for my servant. And your name is Sophia?"

"Yes, sir."

He smiled with approval. "They say His Majesty's favorite daughter has that name."

"Yes, sir," I answered. Though I doubted that was why my parents chose it, I was gratified he liked it.

"How old are you?" he asked.

"Twelve."

"You seem older."

I felt my face flush.

"An only child?"

Though I wished he had *not* said "child," I said, "I am, sir, yes."

He did not seem to notice my hesitation.

"Do you like music?" he asked.

"I do, sir."

"Excellent! I play the flute. I shall be pleased to have you for an audience. And you must know that you are a pretty miss, and someday, if you will give permission, I will make a sketch of you. I have some talent there."

"You are kind," I said, a weak response to his gallant banter.

"And your father," he said. "What occupation does he follow?"

"A scrivener, sir."

"Excellent! A man of letters. Do you read and write, Sophia?"

"Yes, sir. I've read Richardson, Fielding, and—" I almost said Mr. Paine but caught myself.

"Wondersome! You and I shall get on. I must admit, sometimes I try to write poetry." He turned toward the steps and paused to let me go first, which I did.

Mother was in the common room, waiting for us.

The lieutenant said, "A most satisfactory accommodation, madam."

"Will you be moving right in?" she asked.

"As soon as my servant can bring my things. As I said, I've just been released in a prisoner exchange. I don't have very much."

"This servant of yours, will he be staying here too?"

"Peter? Of course." He made a step to the door.

"Sir," said Mother.

John André paused to look at her.

"My husband, Mr. Calderwood, is in bed, in the back room. In all candor, sir, I must tell you he was wounded in the fighting."

A play of sorrow flitted upon the lieutenant's face. "I trust he's in good health?"

"The doctor has seen him."

"I am glad to hear it. Shall we agree that I won't need to know under what circumstance he received his regrettable wound?"

"You are most kind, sir."

He bowed. "I wish you a good evening, madam."

And John André went.

Mother and I exchanged looks of pleasurable surprise. "Perhaps," she said, "we have been lucky."

"He plays music," I said, barely suppressing my newfound enthusiasm. "And draws and likes to read."

Mother studied me. "I think he's already charmed you," she said.

"He asked me if I was an only child."

"What did you say?"

"That I was. Mother," I went on, "he's not at all what I thought he'd be." In truth, I was pixie-led.

Mother looked at me so fixedly, I hurried into the back room to inform Father that Mr. Gaine was not in the city.

"We shall have to be patient." Then he said, "Sophia, it will be you who will need to search for William."

"Why?"

"With this officer lodging here, it might be suspicious if your mother went out too frequently."

"Yes, Father."

"At least we are here and safe. We must be proud—if quiet—that William is defending our liberties."

In my thoughts, however, I was already impatient for the return of the lieutenant. Yet that was the last thing I was prepared to share with my parents. Nor did I tell them how I'd first seen John André.

11

DURING THE NEXT few weeks, things of considerable import happened.

To begin, Father mended so poorly that his right arm and hand were of small use. Dr. Dastuge came a few times, dressed his wound, and replaced the bandage. He also served us with a bill. It was paid, of course, but I heard my parents talk about our sinking funds. It was only what I already knew. After all, Father had not reestablished his means of earning income, and with food prices going up at an alarming rate—some 500 percent!—our money, accordingly, diminished.

Twice Father sent me out in hopes of his being restored to work. Mr. Rivington's shop remained closed. Mr. Gaine had not shown up. Though his servant boy was about, he could tell me nothing about his master's situation, not even if he would come back to the city.

Once, as I was leaving, the servant boy followed me to the door. In a private voice, he asked me if I had seen many sailors on the streets.

"I don't think I did. Why do you ask?"

"They're pressing boys they find on the streets."

"Pressing?"

"Forcing them into their navy. I'm 'fraid to go out."

"Then you must take care," I said, and left him.

There it was; not even young children were safe. But then, all matters of law—trials, courts, judgments—were in the hands of the crude and unfair British military.

While my parents spoke of the absence of Mr. Gaine as unfortunate, I heard Father tell Mother it was just as well—for the time—since he was having much trouble working his hand in a normal fashion. To do his work—edit copy—he would have to use it.

"If he does not recover soon," Mother confided to me, "you may need to hire out as a servant. With all these British officers about, a suitable position might be found."

That was hardly what I would have liked, but if the need came, I knew I could not object.

We did learn that the British had taken so many prisoners they were using the Presbyterian and Dutch churches, Quaker meetinghouses, and even sugar-houses for prisons. I went to all in turn and stood before each, as if to stare at them could provide information. It was, of course, a useless endeavor. As for going to the army headquarters, Father feared telling the authorities that William had fought with the patriots might put us in jeopardy.

In short, we gained no news of William at all.

The other significant event was that Lieutenant

André moved into our house. Along with his servant, a boy of sixteen named Peter Laune, who carried in a large leather-covered, round-topped trunk, they resided on the top floor.

This Peter rarely spoke to me, or to my parents, but lived at the lieutenant's command. He was like André's silent shadow, important only to him.

Strictly speaking, it was the British commandant who should have paid us rent, but the lieutenant was kind enough to pay us out of his own pocket, twenty shillings a week, in good English coin. Given our circumstance, you may guess how appreciated this was.

I knew not what Lieutenant André did for the British Army, but when he was at our home, I found him most agreeable. The courteous mode that he had displayed when he first came to our house did not abate. Talkative, cheerful, and engaging, he played the part of a guest, rather than someone forced upon us. That he was the enemy, the occupying army, I was increasingly willing to put aside.

I was further delighted when he obliged me with stories of his life. I learned that he was twenty-six years old, of French Protestant origins. "But I beg you," he said, "never think me devout."

His father, who had been in trade, had died, leaving him the means to opt for a military life. Well educated, John André was able to speak French and German. He liked to chat about poetry, books, and writing with my father. The two even conversed about the war. Yes, the lieutenant was a fierce and loyal supporter of King

George and his Parliament. Nor did he hide his view that the Americans were not only in the wrong but traitors who must be brought to submission. In truth, his use of the word "American," was meant to be a sly insult, a way of saying the "rebels," as he always called them, were *not* British. Good-naturedly, he accused my father of being a "Leveler," of wanting to make all men equal. Yet, for all that, he talked and debated with Father in an amiable, civilized fashion.

One day he supplied my father, who had yet to leave home, with a copy of the Oath of Allegiance to King George, which, he explained, once signed, would free my family from any inconvenience.

> *This is to certify that* _____
> *hath submitted to government and taken*
> *the Oath of Allegiance to his Majesty King*
> *George this Oct 5, 1776 before me, Jeremiah*
> *Tronson, One of the Judges of the Superior*
> *Court.*

I wondered if Father would put his name in the blank, but he did.

To my mother John André was ever accommodating and polite.

To me he was chivalrous as any imagined prince. Once he even brought me a blue ribbon for my hair, which I was captivated to have. As promised, he entertained me with his flute playing. To my ears he played exceedingly well. He asked Mother if he could make a sketch of me. When she agreed, he found paper and brush pencil somewhere and drew my likeness, which I thought made me appear quite pretty.

"My talent," he informed me, "is showing people as they really are."

I blushed.

In short, having never met so well bred and civilized a man as John André, I was greatly flattered by his attentions. Indeed, I was nothing less than enthralled.

❖ 12 ❖

NEW YORK CITY did not resume what it was. The streets were ever more thronged with enemy soldiers. While there was much orderly marching about, day and night there was rowdiness and drunkenness. Street brawls were frequent. When I was out, I had to become accustomed to vulgarity, aggravation, and insults.

Some mornings, when I went to market, I would see the word "liberty" or "freedom" scrawled on walls, perhaps with bits of burnt wood from the great fire. The words never lasted more than a day, yet would always reappear elsewhere.

Despite all this, going about was vital. It was on the streets that we met our few remaining friends. That enabled us to gather a little news and the rumors of the war. Of course, these exchanges occurred only when out of sight of soldiers.

Thus, in the middle of October, I learned that a battle had been fought on a lake—Champlain—somewhere in the New Hampshire Grants. It seems the British sent a fleet down the lake from Canada to attack our forces and seal off New England. Those ships were met by a navy of our own making. While the English were not defeated, they were checked and forced to retire. I rejoiced.

I further learned that these American forces were under the command of Benedict Arnold, who had captured Montreal and Fort Ticonderoga. A Connecticut man. They said he was so resourceful he had built a navy right in the forest! For once I had an American general to think about with pride. Not that I could speak it.

Then something of like news came from just north of Manhattan (White Plains), where another battle was fought between General Washington's troops and Lord Howe's men. Again, the British, though not overcome, were stopped. My spirits soared.

Nonetheless, the fierce grip the British held upon the city meant that more and more Tories showed up in town, as did loyalist refugees from other colonies. In addition, since the British promised slaves their freedom if they abandoned their patriot masters and came within British lines, large numbers of Negros were on the streets, far more than ever before. With so many people reestablished, city trade began to resume its normal business. But in all things, the army held hard-fisted control.

In short, this was a time of much confusion for me. I was a patriot, eager for good news about our side. I worried constantly about my brother, William. Simultaneously, I was excited by what I took to be the special attentions John André had for me.

He took me to watch the guard changing. He showed

me where Lord Howe was living, at the foot of Broadway. Side by side, we watched Punch and Judy puppets on the street (Punch in an American uniform), and laughingly applauded the Devil (Benjamin Franklin!) dragging Punch to Hell.

André read me poetry, some of it his. He even offered to take me to a soldiers' ball. I was all eagerness, but when he made application to my mother, she, to my mortification, said no. I retreated in a pout.

Let it be admitted: if a twelve-year-old girl has enough heart, it does not take her long to think of herself as being in love. I daresay I liked the thought of myself— for the first time—in such a bemused and pleasant state. Of course, I had no friends left in whom to confide. So I told no one—neither John André nor my mother—of my emotions. Moreover, I allowed myself to think he fancied me. Why, he even wrote a poem for me.

> No matter how young the flower
> Which has yet to burst to bloom,
> The time will come, its finest hour
> When she'll be prettiest in my room.

Simple to be sure, but though I kept it hidden in a secret place, you can imagine how regularly I read it.

Let me be forthright: I was perfectly aware that a war was going on. I considered myself an ardent patriot. Yet, I must confess, I began to think of my brother, William, as a *problem*. What if he—about whom John André knew nothing—suddenly appeared? How would the lieutenant deal with a rebel soldier in our midst?

How would *I* deal with it? Would William attack André? These questions gave me moments of perplexity and confusion. More shame on me! But though William did not appear, in fairness to me, he was frequently in my thoughts.

That said, there I was—a twelve-year-old girl—feeling real affection for one of the enemy. And early affection, as I would learn, lasts late.

❖ 13 ❖

NOVEMBER 1776 CAME, and with it the airborne chill of arriving winter. With still no news about my brother, we began to fear the worst. Perhaps William *had* died in the Brooklyn battle. That being such an awful thing to contemplate, we chose to believe otherwise. After all, if he were safe with General Washington's army, he would have no means of communicating with us. Living in occupied New York, we were quite sealed off from the rest of the country. No, I refused to think him gone. But while I adored my brother, I was aware how much my esteem for John André grew. Though my emotions remained in a state of constant flux, I worked hard to keep them silent. You can imagine my puzzledom!

Then, on the sixteenth of November, we learned that the one place still held by American forces on Manhattan Island—Fort Washington, in the north—had fallen to a fierce British siege.

The news spread rapidly. Some fifty-nine Americans killed. Almost three *thousand* taken prisoner! Now all of Manhattan Island was in British hands. That, the

English wished us to know. Everything for our cause seemed to be going ill.

Though I had heard on the streets the news of the fort's surrender, John André took pleasure in telling us about it. He went further, assuring us that the war would be over soon and all political disputes settled in a proper, legal fashion. Britain would be supreme again. The king's peace would be the order of the day. "How much better for everyone," he proclaimed.

Wishing to offer a mild tease, I rejoined, "Perhaps we'll have our Arnold come down Hudson's River and chase you all away."

"Arnold?" he replied. "Who is he?"

"Our general who captured Montreal, as well as Fort Ticonderoga, and then kept your navy in check on that northern lake."

"I assure you, Miss Calderwood," André replied in perfect humor, "I don't know who this Arnold fellow is, but we shall prevail."

I said no more. Though I would not admit it to anyone, I worried that he was right.

That night, however, he did say one other thing to me. We were alone in the common room. He had been playing his flute, and I was listening with appreciation. When he'd finished, I complimented him on his playing.

"I'm much obliged," he told me. "But, Miss Calderwood, may I be frank with you?"

My heart fluttered. "You may."

"You spoke of your admiration of that rebel general. 'Our general,' you said."

It took me a moment to catch his drift. "Arnold?"

"His name does not signify. I know you spoke with badinage, but I should advise you, such talk is taken seriously by my superiors. Respect for traitors is a grave matter. You must not, Miss Calderwood, let even one taint of this rebellion stain you. It could cause you and your family much harm."

I felt myself go red in the face. Yet I took his warning to heart and was doubly relieved that we had said nothing about William. At the same time, the lieutenant's thoughtful caution made me admire him only more. Was he not protecting me?

I wanted to keep my heart locked tight. It took work. While aware that William was still missing— and the danger he posed for us—I thought of him less and less, while thinking increasingly about handsome, sociable, and charming Lieutenant John André. In short, I was joyful—in a blind way. I gave almost no thought to the future, as if nothing bad could happen.

Dear Reader, do not lose faith in me! I believed in our noble struggle. Every day I reminded myself I was a patriot. Still, there *were* things about which I feared. I knew our store of money kept diminishing. My father was not fully recovered. Mother was constantly worried. In fact, one day early in December, she called me into the back room.

As I stood beside the bed, Father told me that I must go again and see if Mr. Gaine had come back. The same for Mr. Rivington. If they had, I must beg to inquire if

there would be any work for him in the offering. He put
a stress on "beg."

"Are we so short of money?" I asked.

"I fear so," said Father.

"And if he asks about your condition?"

"Say I have been ill."

"And," my mother cautioned yet again, "nothing
about William."

"Of course."

When I told John André that I needed to go to Hanover
Square, he obligingly offered to accompany me. To be
sure, I was more than delighted to be stepping about
town with the lieutenant.

Consider my happiness: me, an altogether smit-
ten girl, *his* blue ribbon in my hair—worn like a love
token—walking about town on the arm of a handsome
officer in a smart red uniform. *What an elegant pair*,
thought I. You may believe me when I say I felt as if my
whole world was that moment.

The lieutenant and I were thus walking along Broad
Street in the North Ward when we came upon a troop
of men herded on by armed redcoats. Since Fort
Washington had recently fallen, I supposed these men
were prisoners from that rout.

These prisoners—some forty men—were the image
of defeat: scrawny, foul, and bandaged. Their cheer-
less faces showed broken spirits, with no light of eye or
smile on any face I saw.

Since they were passing right before us—in the
street—our way was blocked. Of course, it was only

natural that I cast my eye upon them, not in any thoughtful way, but merely out of curiosity. As I recall, John André even made a jest at their expense, which, let it be admitted, made me giggle.

But even as I did, I saw my brother.

❖ 14 ❖

AT FIRST I was not even sure it *was* he. I had to look extra hard, for the face I saw was besmeared with filth, and his clothing soiled and torn. There was, moreover, a cloth wrapped round his right thigh. He limped. Overall, this person was in a deplorable state.

It took moments of stupefied gawking for me to become convinced it *was* my brother, William. Horrified, I wanted to shout his name, but I held myself back because I was standing right next to John André. Had I not been told by both my parents that the lieutenant must know *nothing* about William? Had *he* not said as much? Was that not what *I* had wished? There was something so much more bitter: the truth is that I, for that moment, wished I *had* no brother.

Pushing away such vile thoughts, my heart beating painfully, I could only stare.

"Is something the matter?" I heard John André ask as if from across the sea.

"Who are they?" I murmured, not having wits to know what else to say.

"Prisoners."

"What . . . what will happen to them?" I stammered.

"These men have rebelled against their lawful government" was his reply. "They must pay the penalty for their stupidity. By the laws of all countries, rebels taken in arms forfeit their lives. They will be treated no better than they deserve."

"What do you mean?" I said, taken aback by his harshness.

"They should all be hung."

"*Hung!*" I cried. Upon the instant, my mind filled with the ghastly image of Nathan Hale, which cojoined with that of my brother.

"But they have only sought to defend our liberties," I heard myself say, echoing a phrase Father had used. That I, too, had thought. Indeed, before I could think of what I was saying, I blurted out, "As my brother has."

John André gazed upon me with bepuzzlement.

Realizing what I had done, I turned from him, aghast.

Then I heard him say, "Miss Calderwood, are you saying you have a *brother*?"

My blunder made me afraid to speak or even glance at him. I was equally fearful to look, as it were, at myself. *Who am I? What was I thinking?* I did not know how to respond. Or what to do. By this time, the prisoners had moved farther down the street.

"Miss Calderwood," André pressed, "am I to understand you have a *brother* fighting for the rebels?"

I stood there mute.

"Come, come, Miss Calderwood, rebellion does not suit you," he said in his lighthearted fashion. "Let grown *men* take care of such matters. A maid should not pay any mind to disputed politics."

Unable to look at him, I said, "And what . . . what should a maid put her mind to?"

He boldly turned me about so I had to face him. "To making yourself as agreeable to *me* as possible," he said. "That's the proper employment for a fair young lady. As for a brother, a *rebel* brother"—he gave me his most brilliant smile—"let's agree I did not hear you speak. We shall ignore him."

Flabbergasted—how could I ignore my brother!—I said nothing, but gaped at André as if he were a stranger.

"Miss Calderwood," he went on, "you have my promise: I shall not say one word to your esteemed parents. Or," he added meaningfully, "to the authorities."

As I stood there, I recalled the first time I had seen Lieutenant André. The time when he'd struck that poor, dawdling prisoner with his sword. His words and that memory reminded me that John André was our *enemy*. Further, I recalled who *I* was: *his* enemy, enemy to *his* army, *his* government. And I remembered what *I* was, what he had mockingly called "American."

These thoughts came upon me like blinding bursts of cannon shot so that I could only retreat. "Forgive me," I managed to say, "I must go."

Whirling about, I began to hurry down the street in the same direction taken by the prisoners. I needed to see where William was going.

Even as I went, I was aware that the lieutenant stayed in step with me. I paid him no mind. But after some moments, he reached out, gently touched my arm, and said, "Miss Calderwood, I fear I have offended you by my words. Your brother means nothing to me."

"But, sir," I cried, my voice ragged with emotion, my eyes streaming, "he means everything to me." At the same time I shrugged off his touch, which only moments before I would have treasured.

"You must forgive me," he said.

Somehow, I retorted, "You only spoke your mind, sir."

"Miss Calderwood," he insisted, "please be assured I did not mean to say anything to suggest I don't esteem you."

"Thank you for your company. I can find my own way now."

"Hanover Square is this way." He pointed in a direction opposite where I was heading.

Making no reply, I kept on after the prisoners.

He halted, but called, "I look to see you at home, Miss Calderwood. 'Pon my honor, I'll be more civil with my tongue and opinions."

I hurried after the prisoners.

Moments later, I stopped and watched the lieutenant sauntering away. My primary thought was *I have put my family in peril.* Then, not sure what else to do, I turned and fairly ran in the same direction that I saw my brother—and the other prisoners—go.

⋆ 15 ⋆

AS THE MEN moved slowly down the center of the street, I hurried alongside, searching for another glimpse of my brother. When I saw him, I shouted, "William!"

Some heads—not his—shifted.

"William!" I cried again, in as loud and unladylike a voice as I could muster. "William! It's me! Sophia!"

That time he turned and looked about.

"Here!" I shouted, and raised my hand.

His face blossomed into some life.

"Where are they taking you?" I shouted.

Before he could respond, one of the soldiers came up to him and, with the butt of his musket, struck him on the shoulder.

As William stumbled, I stifled the scream in my throat. It was only because he was caught by one of his fellow prisoners that he did not fall. The soldier who hit him turned toward me. "Go home, girl!"

I had the wits to let the line of prisoners pass. But only briefly. Short of breath, heart racing, greatly disconcerted, I began to follow again, this time making sure I stayed behind the prisoners.

The column of captives proceeded north, going to the west of the Commons area, until they reached the block between Murray and Barclay. They were, I now grasped, going to the King's College, a wide, tall building, with an elegant cupola top center. It was where William had been going to school before hostilities had begun in earnest. Now it was surrounded by soldiers. And the prisoners, including William, were being shoved inside. His school was to become his prison.

I stood for a while outside the ring of guards feeling altogether hurly-burly but trying to regain my composure. All I knew was that I must do something to help my brother. Would they let me visit? Could I bring him food? Would they allow him a doctor?

My next thought was to hasten home and inform my parents about what I had learned. No doubt they would be both greatly relieved and deeply worried—just as I was.

That said, I knew I needed to settle myself. I decided the best way to do so would be to go on to Hanover Square and inquire about Mr. Gaine, as Father had asked me to do. Off I set, relieved to be alone, though my thoughts were as crowded as an unruly mob.

As I went, I kept thinking about William and his suffering. Yet I must admit, I was also thinking of myself, mortified that I had allowed myself to foolishly, and childishly, be distracted by John André. I was reminded of the old adage: Nothing makes one older than knowing how young you are.

Upon reaching Hanover Square, I turned to the sign

of the Bible and crown, Mr. Gaine's printing shop. To my joy, he was there standing before his type case, filling a composing stick with letters.

"Ah, Miss Calderwood," he said as soon as he saw me. "I'm surely delighted to see you. Where has your father been now? I've need of him."

Mr. Hugh Gaine was a short, stocky, round-faced, and stub-nosed man of some fifty years. Though he had been in America for a goodly while, he spoke with a strong Northern Irish accent. It was said that he was a successful man, yet I never saw him dressed other than in the simplest fashion, a suit of brown homespun cloth.

This morning he wore no jacket but had on his leather work apron. I also noticed he had a red ribbon on his arm.

"Mr. Gaine," I said. "My father sends his compliments. He's been ill. But he's close to recovery and wants me to tell you he's eager for employment. I've inquired here a number of times."

"I've been to Jersey, Miss Calderwood. But I am back." He peered about his work space, as if to see who might hear him. I saw no one, not even his servant boy.

"Now you must inform your father," he said loudly—perhaps wishing the world to hear—"that I have seen the way the river is flowing. That's to say, I've convinced those who must be convinced—the British military authorities—that I'm eager for the restoration of His Majesty's government in New York, and in all the colonies. In turn, they have graciously given me permission to continue printing the *Mercury*. I don't presume to know your father's thinking about such matters, Miss Calderwood, but he'll be needing to know mine."

As he spoke, he was looking at me in such a fashion, tipping a nod here, a blink there, that seemed to suggest the opposite of his words. But in those days, it was common for New Yorkers to act in just this contradictory fashion, some nicknackery or trick to suggest opposing minds. In other words, while Mr. Gaine was telling me he was now a loyalist, he was signaling the suggestion that he was still a patriot.

Was this not what my parents had done? Was this not what *I* had done? Dear God! The war made deception our way of life.

That said, I had to make a quick decision: my father needed employment.

"I'm sure he will grasp your meaning, sir," I replied, trying to be as fuzzy as he. "Then do you have work for my father?"

"If he would be so kind." Mr. Gaine went to a table, upon which lay a scattering of papers. He gathered them up and handed them to me. "He can edit these advertisements left for publication. My usual rates."

"Thank you, sir," I said, and took them, certain that my father would be pleased. I turned to go.

"Miss Calderwood!"

I stopped.

"Your father once told me you write and read well. Am I correct?"

"Yes, sir. My brother taught me," I said.

"Miss Calderwood, I had an apprentice. A boy. When I was restored to my home, I found that he had been pressed."

"Sir?"

"Taken up and forced to join their navy."

It was exactly what the boy had feared. "I'm sorry, sir."

"A common practice. Nothing I, or anyone, can do about it. My problem, Miss Calderwood, is that there are few boys—boys who can read and write—left in the city to do the work. If I employ another, he too shall likely be taken. God's truth: it's difficult to do my printing with just two hands.

"What I'm saying, Miss Calderwood, is this: Would you be willing to take on such a position? To be sure, unusual for a girl, but it's to my knowing that there's already been a woman printer down in Williamsburg, Virginia. I can instruct you. Say the word and I'll discuss the details with your father."

Though completely surprised by his suggestion, I was gratified. If Father gave his approval, it would mean more money for our household. "I'll tell my father what you've proposed," I said, bobbing a curtsy.

"Do so soon," he said, and turned back to his work at the type cases.

I headed for home. The notion of being employed in such a fashion had never entered my head. But, as Mr. Gaine said, these were unusual times. I recalled, too, my mother telling me our need was such that I might have to take work as a house servant in a British officer's home. To me, an inky printer's shop would be preferable.

I glanced at the papers Mr. Gaine had given me. I could read them perfectly well and knew how my father would make them compact, ready for the press. Even if Father were not well enough to work on them, I could. As for the other employment promised in his shop, I was not sure what the tasks would be, but I'd not be shy. Learning a trade had to be useful for me. But mostly, if there was more money for us, there would be more money to help free William.

· 16 ·

THE NEARER I came to home, the more disordered my feelings. Was it excitement or distress? Excitement to have seen William alive. Agony at his condition. Misery, too, that John André might be at home. Though I was certain I could rely upon his promise that he would make no problems for my family regarding William, I had no desire to see him.

Fortunately, when I stepped into the house, he was absent and I was able to rush to the back room. My father was abed, my mother in a chair beside him.

"I saw William!" I cried, and revealed all I had discovered.

But—not one word about John André.

The news that William was alive made it easier for my parents to hear the awful things about his condition.

"I suppose he must have been at Fort Washington," said Father.

"But what will happen to him now?" Mother said, as much to herself as to us.

For a moment no one spoke. Then Father said,

"Perhaps we could ask Lieutenant André for assistance when he gets home."

Mother said, "But he knows nothing about William."

That's when I forced myself to say, "He does know."

"How?" my father demanded.

Reluctantly, I told them what had happened when I saw William on the street. At first their response was to say nothing but to look intently at me, so that I hardly knew what to make of their thoughts. Was it censure or sympathy?

But all Father said was, "Perhaps the lieutenant's knowledge is for the best. Did he truly say he'd act as if you had not spoken?"

I nodded.

Mother turned to Father. "Then perhaps you *should* ask his assistance," she said. "He has been a guest in our house."

I thought, *Not really a guest*.

"I will," said Father. "As a gentleman, he can hardly refuse."

"At the least," said Mother, "he can find a way for us to visit William."

I, however, remembered what John André had told me, that William—along with all rebels—should be hung. Too frightened to quote his words, I only said, "There are soldiers all around the college."

"Hopefully one can pass a coin to a guard to gain admittance," said Father. "It's common practice."

Mother, more bluntly, said, "Do we have the money for a bribe?"

Her words were the perfect prompt for me to say, "There *is* some good news. I found Mr. Gaine at his shop."

"Excellent," said Father. "What did he say? Is there any work?"

I held up the papers. "He wants you to take these advertisements and reduce them. The usual rates, he said to tell you."

When Father put out his good hand, I gave him the papers. After a quick perusal, he said to me, "With your help, we'll do them easily."

Then—with hesitation—I told my parents that Mr. Gaine wished to employ me.

Mother immediately expressed her astonishment and doubts, but Father took to it more kindly. There was discussion between them as to whether it was a proper thing for a girl to do such work. For my part, I reminded them we needed more money if we were going to help William.

Father, breaking into a rare smile, said, "Then it will be as Mr. Paine wrote, 'Our new nation is a blank sheet for us to write upon.' And who shall do that better than a girl printer? You must tell Mr. Gaine that if he calls, I'm willing to discuss the matter."

In a matter of two hours, my father and I had completed all Mr. Gaine's notices. I planned to take the rewritten advertisements back to the printer the next day and, hopefully, collect our payment.

"Between Lieutenant André and some ready money, we're sure to free William," Mother said.

Please, God, I thought. *Make it so*.

❖ 17 ❖

THAT EVENING A frost came, along with damp cold that promised snow. Father, weary with pain, gave up waiting for the lieutenant and went to sleep. Mother and I stayed by the fire. We had been talking about William. Mother, having convinced herself that John André was going to provide assistance, was much more at ease. I was not about to share my forebodings.

There was a lull in our conversation, after which Mother suddenly said, "Sophia, there is something I need to say to you about Lieutenant André."

"What about him?"

Mother made me wait while she appeared to shape her words. "You are twelve years old, a child, I would say," she began. "But a young woman, nonetheless." She paused, and in the interval I could feel myself growing warm—not from the fire, but with discomfort. "It is wonderful that the lieutenant will help us," she said. "But, Sophia, you are showing a reckless infatuation with him."

"A what?"

"A misplaced affection. I must say it's neither proper

nor intelligent. Consider your age. Our situation. His position."

Even as I bowed my head, I knew my cheeks were crimson.

She patted my hand gently. "Though we will be extra grateful to him when he helps William, there will be a better time, place, and other persons upon which you can bestow your affections."

"I assure you," I spoke the lie. "I have none for him."

"I'm pleased to hear it." She took my hand and held it, as if to remind me that I was still a child. "But be careful," she whispered. "Young women are severely judged."

We sat there in quietude, during which time I thought of her words. Even as I knew she was right, I resented the notion that she treated my emotions as childish. I sought some gratification in that she used the words "young woman" to describe me.

In the midst of the stillness, there was a sharp rap upon the outside door. Next moment John André, along with his servant, entered the house.

18

"LADIES," CALLED THE lieutenant cheerfully as he and his servant stamped their boots and rubbed hands together, "I wish you a good evening. It's pleasing to have a fire." Snow was on his shoulders.

Both Mother and I had risen when they came in, and she dutifully replied to the lieutenant's greeting. Full of unease, I kept my eyes upon the ground but could not avoid peeking up at him. He was gazing only at Mother. *Is he keeping himself from looking at me?*

He must have sensed our mood, for he said, "Is something amiss?"

"Mr. Calderwood would like to speak to you in the morning."

"I shall wait upon him. But, ladies, I have some wretched news. Wretched for me, at least."

I looked up, startled.

"I've been transferred to Staten Island. That's where most of the green-coated Hessian troops are. With my knowledge of German, I'm needed there. In short, I must be leaving your house."

My release of tension upon hearing this news was

followed by pain and regret. Was the removal *his* choice? Was it because he had learned about William? In an instant, I told myself he had real affection for me, and that this was his way of removing himself from our painful situation. That he was being considerate. Next moment I was sure he was merely removing himself from any connection with rebels. Forcing myself to look at him, I smiled warmly the way all women are taught to do.

When John André glanced in my direction, I tried to read his eyes. He turned away, so I chose to think that had been his way of assuring me we had a secret and it was safe. It was so like the books I'd read: true affection always has obstacles to overcome.

Mother made a short speech about how sorry she was to hear his news.

André thanked her and said he was required to say that no doubt another officer would come and take his place. The housing shortage remained acute.

"Will you be leaving soon?" Mother asked.

"Very soon. I won't go without speaking to Mr. Calderwood. And I give you my pledge, if there is anything I can do for you, you need only ask."

As he spoke these precise words, André glanced at me, which I chose to interpret as an offer to help William.

He made a chivalrous bow and bade us a good night. Just as he went up the steps, he paused to look to me again. *Significantly*, I thought.

Which is why, though in fact he *said* nothing, I had

bravado enough to call, "Lieutenant, is there anything that has made you regret your staying here?"

That wonderful smile. "I assure you, Miss Calderwood, nothing. Quite the contrary." That said, he bowed toward me, and then he and his servant were up the steps and out of sight.

As soon as he was gone, Mother turned to me. "There," she said with enthusiasm. "He's pledged to help William."

I could only nod my agreement and turn away, so she would not see the tears of gratitude welling in my eyes. If John André did that, I would forgive him anything.

"It's time for bed," she said. "Will you bank the fire?" She left the room, tactfully giving me time to compose myself. Ah, she knew me well.

Grateful for her consideration, I knelt to work the coals into a smoldering heap so that they would remain until morning. In my state, I hardly knew what to do with the emotions I had for John André. No wonder that I made a metaphor of what I was doing: I would bank my fires of affection for John André, and wait for such day and time that I could allow them to burst into flame again.

I retrieved my blue ribbon and poem from their hiding place, a tin box in which I kept old flower petals, flowers he had once brought. I meant to throw all into the fire. Instead, after gazing at each item, I returned them to the box.

Moreover, I promised myself that starting the next day I would do everything in my power to assist my brother. As for John André, I would put aside—for now—any affection I had for him. If there is such a thing as pleasurable regret, I had it.

Ah, I blush to tell it so! But I have promised you honesty, Dear Reader, and I shall hold to it.

❖ 19 ❖

IN THE MORNING, not wanting to see John André, I left our house as soon as was convenient to Mother. Bundled in a wool cape against the frost, the rewritten advertisement papers clutched in hand, I headed for Hanover Square and Mr. Gaine.

Overhead the sky was gray, and an inch of white snow lay upon the ground. It softened the town's hard edges, hid the mud, and muffled sharp sounds. People on the streets walked in haste, hands pinked with cold, white mists of breath before their mouths. Footprints on the streets reminded me of black currants on a one-penny bun. But now and again a scarlet-coated soldier hastened by, which put me in mind of my brother's wound.

I had not gone far when I happened to meet a friend of Mother's, Mistress Lorenz, a harmless gossip. It would have been rude not to pause and greet her.

"Good morning, madam," I said.

"And to you too, Miss Calderwood. Any news of your brother?"

Not aware what, if anything, Mother had told her, I said only, "Nothing."

"I've heard say," she confided, "that General Washington is retreating across Jersey. Perhaps William is with him. Let's pray he's not a prisoner." She leaned closer. "They say conditions are shocking." Perhaps I paled, for she showed smug satisfaction at having educated me. Pressing my arm and mumbling, "My compliments to your mother, Miss Calderwood," she went off.

I rushed on, not wishing to study her words. As it turned out, Mr. Gaine was in his shop, working his press, concentrating so that he did not notice me when I stood at the door. I watched him with interest, wondering what duties he would give me.

"Mr. Gaine," I finally said, "good day."

"Ah, Miss Calderwood. I'm positively delighted to see you."

"My father's compliments, sir. He's done these for you." I handed him the revised advertisements.

Mr. Gaine wiped his ink-stained hands upon his leather apron, took the papers, and leafed through them. "Excellent." Then he considered me with a look of expectation. "And you, Miss Calderwood," he said. "Did you discuss my offer of employment with your da?"

"I should be pleased to enter your service, Mr. Gaine. Father said you should call upon him soon."

"Good news indeed! I'll go today." Mr. Gaine turned to a box, opened the lid, and took out some shilling pieces, which he handed to me. "Forgive me for presenting *you* with your father's payment, Miss Calderwood. But I know ready money is in demand."

"It's appreciated, Mr. Gaine," I said, hoping he would not always be so stiff and formal.

We made our farewells. Then, with the coins held tightly in hand, I headed north toward the King's College and, hopefully, William.

✦ 20 ✦

DESPITE THE SNOW, it did not take me long to reach the college building. A large number of armed soldiers surrounded it, like a living, insurmountable wall. Knowing that it had become a prison, I could no longer think of it as a place of learning. Quite the opposite. Moreover, as I gazed upon the building's rows of windows, I fancied I could see many people inside. Too many. Even from a distance, I observed inmates crowding and pressing against the windows, as if seeking air. From one window, a hand reached out, like that of someone drowning in the sea.

In the off chance I'd be able to catch a glimpse of William at a window, I drew nearer. Even as I watched, a troop of soldiers, led by officers, emerged from the central door. With disgust, I saw the same portly, red-nosed officer who had marched Nathan Hale to his death leading the way. His lumbering stride was heavy and gross.

I knew his rank and name now—Provost Cunningham—and had learned his history. He had been abused by the Sons of Liberty—was William one of them?—and was now revenging the favor multitimes. Thus does cruelty beget cruelty.

Afraid he would recognize me, I shrank back, but he passed without so much as a glance in my direction. Nonetheless, just to see him gave me a chill harsher than the cold air did.

Seeing the provost reminded me of my brother's possible fate, and my fears redoubled. Indeed, John André's words "By the laws of all countries, rebels taken in arms forfeit their lives. They should all be hung" were more than menacing. What if the lieutenant refused to intercede?

With my anxiety telling me that I must act in haste, I clutched my coins tightly and stepped forward. As I went, I tried to decide which of the soldiers I should approach. By that time I had seen so many British soldiers I could read their uniforms. That is to say, I knew which ones were common soldiers, which officers. John André had told me that British officers purchased their commissions. Therefore, since officers were most likely gentlemen, my innocence suggested they would be less inclined to take a bribe. Such reasoning suggested a lower-grade soldier would have more need and be more inclined to help me. So I scanned the line of guards and picked out a young soldier.

He was about the same age as William, with red cheeks and flaxen hair beneath his tall hat. On his shoulder was a musket with a bayonet, taller than he was. As I drew closer, he came to attention.

"Yes, miss," he said, standing stiffly. "Good morning. You can't come any further, miss."

"I know, sir. But I'm searching for my brother. I saw him led into the building, a prisoner."

"Sorry, miss. Can't rightly help you."

"Is there a way to be sure he's here?"

"Miss, there are some five thousand prisoners in the city."

I did not move.

The soldier sighed. "The sergeant down the line, miss. He's got a ledger, but under orders from Provost Cunningham, he's not to give out names."

"Is it something you can determine, sir?"

"Not usually, miss."

I held out my hand. The two shilling pieces Mr. Gaine had given me rested in my palm. "It would be a kindness, sir."

He stood still, as if considering my request. I observed his eyes move, first to my hand, then along the line of soldiers as if trying to determine if he was being watched.

"Step closer, miss," he said in an undertone.

I did so, my hand out.

Quick as a flea jump, his free hand snatched the coins.

"What's his name?" he asked.

"William. William Calderwood."

"Back off," said the soldier, "as if going away."

I retreated some yards. He stood where he had been until I wondered if he was going to do as I asked. Then he shifted and marched down along the line of guards before stopping in front of a man I took to be an officer. They seemed to confer. Their hands touched. I suspect shillings were divided. The officer opened what appeared to be a book.

Back came my soldier. I waited for a few moments, then approached.

When I drew near, he spoke in a low voice to say, "He's been transferred to the sugarhouse on Crown Street."

I had no choice but to walk away. My only thought was *John André* must *help us*.

21

HOME AGAIN AND by my father's bed, the first thing I asked was "Did you speak to Lieutenant André?"

"Not yet."

I told them what I had learned about William, after which Father said, "When I speak to the lieutenant, I'm sure he'll at least arrange a visit. We'll bring food. Dr. Dastuge." He lowered his voice. "Find a way to free him."

In the end, however, I had to tell them that whatever we did—even with John André's help—I had little doubt it would take lots of money. Had I not given all Mr. Gaine gave me just to get information?

Mother said, "Lieutenant André said someone would take his place. But that officer is not likely to be so forthright in his payments."

"Here's some good fortune," said Father. "While you were gone, Mr. Gaine stepped by. He and I agreed to terms and conditions for your employment. Five shillings the day. He expects to see you tomorrow."

"Hopefully," said Mother, "that money will be sufficient."

I surely desired it. But even more than that, I counted

on John André's words, "If there is anything I can do for you, you need only ask."

Which meant there was nothing to do but wait for Father to speak to him.

✦ 22 ✦

AS IT HAPPENED, that night the lieutenant came home late, so there was no talk. The next day, I left early for Mr. Gaine's printing shop, where my training as a printer commenced. Thus, I learned about type cases, type racks, the difference between upper and lower case letters, composing sticks, forms, wetting troughs, and quoins. I came to learn such a word as "galley," the difference between "puller" and "beater," how to ink type, plus a veritable encyclopedia of other words and tasks too numerous to list.

Though hard and inky work, it was never drudgery. I liked it. Moreover, Mr. Gaine was impressed—he said so—by my quickness and willingness to learn. So it was that on that first day I went home weary but content. The knowledge that I was earning money, which could help William, gave added pleasure. For the moment I could think of nothing else.

But when I stepped into my house, I was taken aback by the sight of Lieutenant André's large trunk in the middle of the common room. Sitting on it was his servant, Peter.

Although I had tried to put aside all tender sentiments regarding John André, I will be honest and say that when I saw the trunk and understood that he was about to go, my heart tumbled.

"Is your master leaving now?" I asked Peter.

"He is saying his farewells to your parents" was the answer. The young man somehow hoisted the large trunk upon his back and left the house.

I knew what I could have done. Should have done. Gone into the back bedroom and made my respectful farewells along with my parents. If, as I assumed would be the case, John André offered some help concerning William, I should be there to thank him too.

Instead I remained where I was, opting for a romantical meeting with him—alone.

I had some while to wait, which I did with rising agitation. Might it be better to avoid him? Was I not confused enough about my feelings toward him as it were? As proof of my bewilderment, I did nothing. At length the inner door opened and André appeared. His look was serious, to which his dark complexion, black hair, and strong eyes gave a somber cast. When he gazed around, however, and saw me, his face brightened. That easy, frank smile, which I had come so much to admire, flashed upon me like new light.

"Miss Calderwood!" he exclaimed. "I am delighted to see you, indeed. I was afraid I was going to miss you."

"Then you are really leaving?" I said, which, overall, was as dull a remark as one could make.

"Taken to Staten Island this very night. I was just paying my respects to your parents."

There followed a moment of awkwardness. I did wonder that my parents did not follow him. The realization that they had not gave me unease.

"Did my parents ask . . . ?" I faltered.

"Did they request my help regarding your unfortunate brother?"

I nodded.

"They did, Miss Calderwood. They did." He paused.

I tried to read the small smile on his lips. Was it pleasure? Mockery? Sadness? Why would he not speak? "And?" I forced myself to say.

"Miss Calderwood, I beg you to comprehend the delicacy of my situation. I am the eldest son of my family, and with my father deceased, I am responsible for my relations: mother, three sisters, and a younger brother, whose name, by the by, is also William. In short, Miss Calderwood, I must not let the slightest hint of irregularity brush against my honor as a British officer. That honor is the most important thing in my life.

"I assure you, Miss Calderwood, my positing to Staten Island is pure coincidence but, given the circumstance, you must agree, fortunate for all."

I added other meanings to his words but said only, "Can you not get—as you did for my father—an allegiance form for my brother?"

"I fear he has already taken up arms against the government."

"Then you won't help?"

"No."

"But, lieutenant, you pledged to—"

"Miss Calderwood, I cannot."

To hear that was as much to say "There shall be no more daylight."

Struggling for words, I said, "Lieutenant André, may I, may I remind you what you said to me, 'I give you my pledge. If there is anything I can do for you, you need only ask.'"

He was silent for a moment. Then, no longer smiling, he replied, "Miss Calderwood, can I in turn remind you of your age, which, I believe, is merely twelve. A promise to a girl is *not* a pledge to a lady. You are not yet a lady."

Then he made a curt bow and left the house, leaving me alone with profound humiliation and rage.

Immediately, *I* made a pledge: lady or no, *I* would rescue William.

❖ 23 ❖

FIRST, HOWEVER, I needed to visit him. Since I had already gained some knowledge of what amount of bribe it would take to accomplish that, I believed it good fortune—in every sense—that Mr. Gaine had employed me. So it was that I went to his shop each day. It meant money in hand, highly valued British coin. That said, it was going to take time to earn what I thought would be required. Fortunately, while I worked, I also brought home advertisements for Father to edit.

On a number of occasions after my day's work, I went to the sugarhouse situated near Crown and Nassau Streets. It was close to a Dutch church and its adjacent graveyard. Until recently it had been used for the refining of Jamaican sugar; hence its name. Having been built like a fortress, with large stones to make it fire-proof, it is hardly a wonder that the British converted it to a prison. Five stories high, it had small, deep-set windows covered with gratings, and but one entryway, a small, barred door on the Crown Street side.

Though there was no light within, I stood before it. Futile, of course. Yet I wanted to think that William's face was one of those pressing at a window and that he saw me.

I remained for a while, then left.

At home Father continued to mend, if poorly. He got out of bed. He walked about. Though his arm and hand remained stiff and awkward in their movements, he made no complaint. Nonetheless, he stayed at home. While he did not say as much, I believed he thought that if he was seen and his wound noticed, there was the chance of his being arrested.

General Washington, as much as anyone knew, had hidden his small army somewhere in Pennsylvania. It's no wonder the British were convinced the war was all but over. Indeed, our Congress, anticipating an attack on Philadelphia, fled to the city of Baltimore. Nevertheless, a confident Lord Howe chose to stay in New York and settled into winter quarters.

I'll not deny I wished the war would end too, so William would be released. As for John André, I took satisfaction that I did not think of him, but prided myself on *not* thinking.

Then, three days after Christmas, we heard the astonishing news that General Washington had captured the town of Trenton from German troops and went on to *defeat* British troops at Princeton. The patriot cause was alive. Among the few with whom we still communicated, there was elation.

A confession: *I* was not so delighted. I knew what it meant: The war would continue. William was not going to be free. Then I realized I was thinking that the freedom of my country was something less important than the freedom of my brother.

Ashamed of myself, but ever more desperate, I convinced my parents that I should take whatever money we had in hand and make an effort to see William. They agreed to let me try.

I went back to the sugarhouse. As I stood before the building, I watched two armed redcoat guards pass back and forth in front of the door. What a stronghold it was that it took so few guards to secure it!

Filled with apprehension, I gripped my money tightly in hand and stepped forward, waiting until one of the guards drew near.

"Sir!" I called.

The soldier halted and peered down at me but said nothing. An older man, tall and thin, he was what people call a dry-bones. His uniform was ill fitting and his equally wrinkled face bore a hook of a nose, dull eyes, and shaggy eyebrows. I wondered how many years he had been a soldier.

"Please, sir," I said. "I have a brother inside. A prisoner. I am desperate to see him."

"How do you know he's here?"

"A week ago, the guards at the King's College told me so."

The soldier was silent for some moments before he said, "No one is allowed to visit."

I took a breath. "Would some coins help?"

He peeked down at me with those graveyard eyes. "Likely," he allowed.

I stepped forward and held out some forty shillings—more than a week's pay—in my cupped hands. "Will this do?"

He studied the coins but said and did nothing.

Reaching closer, I barely managed to say, "It's all I have, sir."

He lifted his doleful gaze to my face, so that it took all my strength to look back. Then he said, "I got to share it with the other," by which I took him to mean the other guard.

"I beg you, sir, I don't have more."

He was silent for a few more moments before stretching out his hand. When I poured the coins into his large palm, he transferred them to his powder pouch. "What's his name?" he said.

"William Calderwood."

"Follow me," he said with a jerky movement of his head.

I followed him up a few stone steps. Using a large key, he unlocked the heavy door, pushed, and stepped into the sugarhouse.

How sweet the name, sugarhouse. How cruel the reality. For we had entered a dank, murky hallway, where I was immediately assaulted by a suffocating stench of sweat, dirt, and excrement. The ceiling was low. There was no heat. The stone floors were spread with damp and rotten straw. Beyond all else, it was astonishingly crowded with men, far too many for the space, like barely alive fish stuffed into a barrel.

Some men were leaning against the walls. Others sat. Many more lay prostrate on the stone floor. All were foul, with but scant clothing, a few bits looking like old uniforms. What garments they had gave ill comfort against the raw cold and extreme grime. Many had crude bandages. Some were shackled in chains. Even in the murk, I could see bodies shaking, presumably with chills, fever, fear, or all three.

When the guard and I appeared, gaunt, pallid faces turned to me, staring as if *I* were an apparition. Yet it was their faces, ghostlike, that begged for compassion. Not with words. They were as silent as ice.

The guard bellowed, "Girl here for her brother! William Calderwood!"

If they had told me William was dead, it could not have been more appalling than what was the response: *nothing*, nothing at all. Rather, these miserable men merely stared mutely at me with what I translated as wordless entreaties to do *something, anything*, to alleviate their degrading, putrid misery.

Suppressing my impulse to gag, I called, "William! William!" Oh, but my voice was too frail and useless against this storehouse of horrors.

When I received no answer, I had no choice but to wander about, calling, calling. The guard remained at my side.

Each level of the building was divided into two large rooms, with, as I had first observed, low ceilings and naught but dim light seeping through the windows, windows further obscured by bars.

The condition of the prisoners was, at best, horrendous. The scene I'd witnessed when first I entered was repeated everywhere. All was crowded. All was filth, reek, and the cruel calamity of human disintegration and rot.

Constantly calling my brother's name, I had to force myself on. When I received no response, my terror grew.

Where is he?

24

I CALLED WILLIAM'S name many times. But it was not until I reached the fourth floor that I found him. He was in a corner, midst a cluster of other men, grouped as if to share desolation.

He lay on the floor, looking far worse than when I saw him on the street with other prisoners. I could see for myself his thigh wound gave him much pain and was secreting greenish pus.

Indeed, if ever I have observed the face of war, it was William. Body as thin as any fence rail, covered with grime, hair sparse and discolored, eyes red-rimmed, and his youth all leached away. What remained was like a bleached and empty shell upon a barren ocean shore.

For his part, it was as if he did not believe anyone was seeking him. With effort, he pushed himself up on one skeletal elbow.

"Sophia?" he asked like a kitten mewing.

When my soldier guide stepped back with some crude courtesy, I dropped to my knees. William and I embraced. I am not ashamed to say that in our first moments we shared nothing but tears.

In bits and pieces, he told me all that had happened, from the battle in Brooklyn, now months ago, his retreat through Manhattan, his placement in Fort Washington, the siege there. How he was wounded. His capture. "These are some of my comrades," he said, indicating the men around him.

"When we were first taken prisoner," he told me, "the British and German soldiers went round in gangs and stole from us whatever things or comforts we had, even to our shoe buckles. They beat and kicked us repeatedly.

"At King's College, where I was first taken, they stole the bed clothing from those who were ill. There are many with prison fever. Many are dying here. The dead-cart comes and goes every day."

Repeatedly I told him how much he was loved, that we would do everything we could to help him.

To my astonishment, even in that ghastly place, he asked, "Are we winning?"

I told what good news I had, Arnold's check of the British in the north. That General Washington had won great battles in Jersey. I did not tell him that the British had taken Newport.

And what did he say to his companions? "The army is still alive."

In as low a voice as I could manage, I said, "Can one escape?"

"Some have tried. Almost none succeed. It takes strength."

"Is there any way I can help?"

"Food," he said. "We lack food. And decent water."

"I'll be back as soon as I can."

"My love to Father and Mother."

"They are proud of you," I said.

We embraced anew, after which I took my leave.

The soldier guided me out.

"Why do you treat them so cruelly?" I burst out.

He shrugged. "Call them prisoners and they've got rights. Better to call them rebels and say they've none. It's easier." Then he added, "Just know the army commissioners whose job it is to feed them grow fat."

Once outside, I gulped the cold, fresh air as if it were water and I were parched.

I turned to the guard. "Can I bring him food and water?"

He shrugged.

I guessed his meaning. "How much?"

"All you can."

I turned away and started for home.

As if to hide the utter misery of what I had seen, the snow began to fall again. The cold had intensified. I recalled my brother's question, "Are we winning?"

What is winning? I wondered.

As I walked away, the nearby church bell began to peal, as if announcing someone's death. I wept all the way home, my hot tears freezing on my face.

25

THE NEW YEAR, 1777, arrived. It was a year, as someone said, that had three gallows in its name.

It took me a week—the first week of the year—to earn what I thought was the necessary money to bribe my way back into the sugarhouse.

So it was on a Sunday afternoon, after we had gone to services at St. Paul's Church, that Mother filled my handbasket with bread, some meat, and a clay jar of water. At the bottom of the basket lay all the money we had been able to put aside.

The day was much like the others we had been experiencing that early January; rock cold and blustery. Now and again snow swirled, like goose feathers dumped from a pillow. Above, the iron-gray sky hung low. Streets were deserted. The only sound was the munch of snow beneath my boots, like breaking bones.

I had bundled myself as best I could, woolen cape held tight about my throat, cap pulled down, hands so chilled I kept switching them to carry the basket. On my cape, the ribbon of allegiance. *Red*, I thought, *red with shame*. Oh, Desperation, your other name is Deception.

As I approached the sugarhouse, I was hoping the guard with whom I had dealt before would be there. I was not to be disappointed. Even from afar, I recognized his thin, gangly form. I went right to him.

"A good morning to you, sir."

As if he had been in a doze, he started.

"Do you remember me, sir?" I said. "You helped me find my prisoner brother the other day."

"Wondered if you'd come back."

I held up the basket. "I've brought some food for him and if—"

He cut me off. "He's no longer here."

"But where—?"

"I saw him led off to the *Good Intent*."

"Forgive me, sir. I don't know your meaning."

"He's on a prison ship. In Hudson's River."

"But you said, 'the good intent.'"

"A two-masted square rigger. The *Good Intent* is her name. Turned her into a prison ship."

"You jest."

"There's no humor in me, miss."

I stood there in a state of disbelief. "Can I visit this ship?"

"Don't know. She's just off the King's Wharf. It'll take money."

I stood unmoving for a while, dumbfounded, angry, and tormented, all of which rendered me incapable of deciding what to do. Except the aching need to do *something*.

Next moment I whirled about, and with my momentary fury providing me some heat, I clutched my basket and started west and north, toward Hudson's River.

The King's Wharf lay at the foot of Partition Street, somewhat north of where the Jersey Ferry used to run. To get there I had to walk through the burnt ruins of the city fire. In many places, people had patched together crude huts from salvaged timbers and discarded sails, so there were a fair number of tents. The area had even begun to be called "canvas town." It was here that many of the freedom-seeking slaves were forced to live.

Threads of rising smoke suggested little fires for small warmth and cooking. No doubt they used charred remains for fuel. The city was devouring itself.

The King's Wharf jutted into the river. Coils of rope, barrels, baskets, and crates lay about in no order. A rusty and cracked cannon lay on its side. Ships of various sizes—I noticed a sloop and schooner, plus one frigate—were tied to the wharf. Even as I stood there, the wharf creaked and groaned like a sick man.

Beyond lay the wide Hudson's River. In the glumming, Jersey was barely visible. Against the New York shore, clumps of mottled, grit-encrusted ice had formed, while farther out larger chunks floated by like deformed and filthy swans. I wondered if the whole river would freeze, as sometimes happened.

Anchored in the river were more ships, which, by their cannon ports, I knew to be ships of war. Others I supposed were transports. I did see a two-masted brig, which appeared to be in ill repair. I wondered if it was the *Good Intent*, though its appearance dressed it to the contrary. To my eyes, the whole scene was composed of multiple shades of mumpish gray, devoid of any warmth of life, a corpse-colored landscape.

As I approached the dock, I saw several soldiers seated on boxes. These boxes had been set round a large iron kettle, from which, as if some demon were being cooked, fingers of flickering flames reached up.

The soldiers, their ruddy faces reflecting the hellish glow, held out their hands as if to grasp those fiery fingers. Nearby, their muskets stood upright like a gathering of frozen stalks of Indian corn.

I removed the money from the bottom of the basket and put it into a pocket so I could reach it with ease. Then, shivering from cold and raw emotions, my breath a dead mist before my lips, I approached the soldiers. I had to stand off awhile before one of the soldiers even bothered to consider me.

"What say you, miss? You selling something?" He gestured to the basket I was clutching tightly.

"No, sir. It's the prison ship. The *Good Intent*. If it can be visited, I should like to."

"Why?"

"My brother's on it."

The soldiers eyed one another mutely, as if needing to react together.

A soldier asked, "What makes you sure he's on it?"

"I was told by a guard at the Crown Street sugarhouse."

"Is your brother still alive?"

"God a mercy, sir!"

The soldier shrugged. "They die a lot."

"Heaved off like frozen logs," added another.

"I'm sure he's alive," I insisted. When no one spoke, I said, "Is there anyone that can take me?"

"It costs."

"I know, sir."

"If you think its cold here, it's worse there."

Another said, "Anyway, it's growing late. There's not much time."

"Please, sirs. It's my brother."

"What do you have in the basket?" said another.

"Food."

"Willing to be searched, miss?"

"Yes, sir."

They didn't.

One of the soldiers shifted round. "Your brother, you say. How old are you?"

"Twelve, sir."

"I have a sister near that age. I wish she'd come for *me*."

"I beg you, sirs."

No one moved. I just stood there. Then the soldier who had last spoken—who had a sister—stood up with a grunt. "Come along."

"How much shall I give you?"

"Just come," he growled.

I followed.

❖ 26 ❖

WE WENT DOWN some rickety steps toward the water and boarded a small, smutty rowboat. I took my place in the narrow stern seat, while the soldier, oars in his large raw-red hands, sat facing me.

He pushed off.

The river proved choppy enough that I had to cling to my seat. Large chunks of ice floated by, thumping and shuddering our boat, whose prow constantly smacked the water's surface, sending up cold spray, which froze upon me. Now and again the soldier-rower slipped his draw, splashing more water on me. I was quickly wet, trembling, and ever more fearful.

The soldier grunted with each pull of his oars. I dared not say anything, but clutched my basket to control my shakes. The monotonous *slap, slap* of the oars put me in mind of a ticking clock and made me terrified I was too late.

As we drew closer to the *Good Intent*, she loomed ever larger. The flinty-gray color of her hull gave her the appearance of some monstrous dead fish. Indeed, there seemed to be no life about her. She bore no sails. No flags. Icicles dangled from her spars like rows of white shark teeth, while her bow was hung about with frozen sea-weed, which made me think of Neptune's beard. Anchor lines ran from bow and stern. But then, she was not going anywhere. Gun ports were blocked, although a series of small holes had been cut high into her hull.

The soldier said, "Mind, it's late, miss. I can't stay long. No one on board will take you back. You don't want to stay on her, miss. It'll be worth your life. Get off quick as you can. I'll wait."

"I'm grateful for your help."

"You're a brave one. Remind me of my sister, God keep her."

"Where is she?"

A shrug. "Don't know. Five years gone since I seen her last."

When we were very near to the ship, a sailor leaned over the gunwale. "Who's there?" he called in a thick, guttural voice.

My soldier called, "A visitor for a prisoner!"

"It's late."

"She'll hurry."

"*She*? A lady, then?" I could hear the leer.

"Girl."

"*Girl*? Ha! Any money?"

The soldier allowed me to answer, which I did with a quick nod.

"Aye!" my soldier shouted up.

"What's the watchwords?"

"Good health to King George."

"Come on."

27

LIKE A SUCKLING PUP, our boat nudged the looming ship, which towered over me and seemed beyond reach. Next moment a rope ladder *clump*ed down. That I had to climb unnerved me. The thought must have been on my face because my soldier said, "There's no other way, miss. Yes or no?"

"Yes, please."

He grabbed the ladder, held it taut. With our boat pitching and yawing beneath my feet, basket heavy in the crook of my arm, I took hold of the ladder with two hands. Though it was icy cold and slippery, I began to climb.

I went but haltingly. With the ladder swaying constantly and my arms aching, I was sure I must fall. More than once I had to pause and close my eyes, but managed to cling on. When I neared the ladder's top, coarse hands reached down and yanked me roughly the final way. In moments I stood upon the deck, legs wobbly, head dizzy, heart pounding.

Standing there, trying to regain my breath and balance, I was engulfed by the fetid stench of decay. I lifted my eyes and gazed about. All was in disorder, as if the ship's tools, rope, sail, spars, deadeyes, and lanyards had begun to disintegrate. Midst it all, as if similarly undone, were men like those I had seen in the sugarhouse. They lay or sat about in semifrozen stupor, their emaciated, dirty bodies protected with naught but rags. To a man, they appeared deceased and haggard, nearer the shores of death than life.

British soldiers, slovenly in appearance, were standing guard, some with muskets in hand, others with clubs. These ghastly looking men gazed upon me like birds of prey and I a passing morsel.

"What do you want here?" came a harsh voice.

I looked around. Though his jacket proclaimed him an officer, the man was as rantum-scantum as the others.

"I'm asking what do you want here?" came the question again, louder.

"I . . . brought food for my brother." I held up my pathetic basket.

"What's his name?"

"William. William Calderwood."

"You can try and find him." As he spoke, he held out his hand, as if expecting me to give him the basket for permission to look.

I held back.

"If you want to look, you'll need to give that over," he demanded.

I gave it to him.

Then he said, "Money?"

I gave him what I had.

He seemed to calculate the amount. "More?"

"None," I said.

That he kept the basket shocked me, but I did not say anything. A soldier was beckoning.

He led me to an opening on the deck. Off to one side was a wooden grate. Steps—with a kind of side rail— led down into what appeared to be a bottomless pit. I turned to the soldier for instruction.

"If he's anywhere, it's down there."

"Is there no light?"

"What you see."

I was so frightened I could do nothing.

"Step lively," said the solider. "It's getting on to night."

I forced myself to grip the handrail and began to descend into a black hole, from dark to darker, where night itself must sleep.

Halfway down I stopped and stared about. Gradually my eyes grew accustomed to the foul and rotten gloom. What I saw were men sprawled everywhere, entangled like rotting eels. All were in the most desolate conditions of neglect.

This was the sugarhouse, *twice* as horrible. This was not mere disregard and ignorance. This, by multiple degrees, was murder.

I was too frightened to go any farther.

"William," I called out. "William Calderwood!"

No answer.

"William!" I shouted. "William Calderwood!"

No reply. Someone coughed. Groaned. Bodies shifted.

The stench was overwhelming. I thought I heard the sound of retching. Then, from somewhere, I knew not where, a thin voice called, "Who asks?"

"His sister."

"William Calderwood," came the voice, "died two days ago."

28

THOUGH IT WAS pitch night when I was rowed back to shore, it was nothing like the darkness in my heart. I do not know if there were sufficient words in Father's dictionary to give reality to what I saw on the *Good Intent*. Enough to say that if you ever doubted the existence of Hell, I can tell you—it is real. That day I saw it. And as preachers remind us of Hell to shape our destiny, know that the Hell *I* saw shaped mine.

So I trust you will completely accept it when I reveal that in my grief I vowed I would avenge William's awful death. Moreover, I believed that John André had the power to save my brother. But he refused.

By mid-January of 1777, all the rivers around New York were frozen solid. Just as, I believed, was my heart.

Ah! But was that so? You, Dear Reader, must decide.

PART TWO

———

1780

29

THE DEATH OF William proved a terrible blow to my parents and to me. To lose one's only son, heir, and dearest brother to such cruelty is beyond measure. Our suffering was immense. It grew even worse when we could not learn if he had been buried decently—if at all. As it has been said: "To lose a loved one is but part of living life, whereas to have a loved one vanish is a living death."

For a long while my parents remained sunk in plightful melancholy, aging rapidly before my eyes. Yes, over time they resumed a *kind* of being, though much subdued in spirit and strength. Father worked for a number of printers in the city and engaged in some legal copy work. He did it all at home, for one lasting effect of William's death was that my parents almost never walked out. It was I who received and delivered Father's work to various employers and did the marketing for Mother.

But unlike my parents, I would not be defeated. With reports of prisoner deaths in British prisons multiplying, as did the denials, my hatred of the occupying

British Army grew accordingly. Because of William's and Captain Hale's deaths (and all the others'), I wanted to become the soldier my brother had been. My intent was that I would somehow become a warrior in the great battle not yet won.

But it was only three years after William's death—in 1780—a leap year, when I reached the age of fifteen, that I finally had my chance. What I did had vast consequences, which I shall now set forth before you.

30

FIRST, HOWEVER, YOU must know some of the events that followed William's death.

Beyond all else, the war went on. New York City stayed under control of the British Army and remained their headquarters. The first commander in chief was Lord General Howe. From May 1778 forward, it was Sir Henry Clinton.

Because New York was the principal British stronghold in America, the population grew, increased by ever more troops, English, Scot, and German. Tories arrived from all regions of the country. So did freedom-seeking slaves. The city's population, it was claimed, came to exceed thirty thousand.

Many British officers brought wives and children from England to build a regular military establishment. As a result, a lively social life ensued. There was theater, horse races (in Brooklyn), concerts, foxhunts, balls, banquets, and Monday-afternoon games of cricket. All this despite constant fear that General Washington's army was about to attack.

The city's greatest difficulty was securing food.

Rebellious citizens and patriot troops surrounded the city. Nearby Long Island was unable to produce adequate amounts, and marauding British troops and Tory sympathizers could steal only so much. Shortages were such a constant that most food—for the British Army as well as for city citizens—was brought in huge fleets from Cork, Ireland, some three thousand miles away, a voyage of at least one month, and it could take longer.

Now and again these ships came late because of weather, acts of war, or incompetence. Spoilage was as ordinary as theft and graft. Within a brief time, food prices rose like rockets, eight *hundred* percent and beyond. Most citizens suffered terribly. For the thousands of American prisoners in New York—already mistreated and malnourished—it meant death. Only the officers charged with their care grew rich. Indeed, there was an incessant illegal trade of common necessities.

As for the war itself, in October 1777 our patriot army won a major victory over the British at Saratoga, far north of the city. General Benedict Arnold, though wounded, was not just victorious but the hero. In so doing, he once again proved himself the ablest commander in the patriot army. Had he not won in Montreal, Ticonderoga, and Lake Champlain and forced a huge British Army to surrender in Saratoga? His triumph brought a vital alliance with France.

I told my father if we had two Benedict Arnolds, America could win the war.

"At least we have the one," he replied. "And we have Washington."

"My hero," I replied, "is General Arnold."

Yet, to be truthful, during this same three-year period, American forces suffered defeats at Brandywine, Germantown, Monmouth, Savannah, and Augusta. All of Georgia was lost until we struck back at Kettle Creek and Stony Point. At one point, even Philadelphia was given up. Congress had to flee, but settled there again when Lord General Howe retreated from the city.

In other words, although the patriot cause was not lost, it was not winning. Thus, in 1780, the struggle for independence still swung upon the hinge of history. The door to liberty was neither open nor shut, and though I knew it not, I would have my hand on that door.

Over these three years, *I* changed. Taller. Fuller. More a young lady than a girl. If you think I speak from vanity, Mother herself exclaimed, "Your brother would not recognize you now."

There would be more he would not recognize.

31

AFTER LIEUTENANT ANDRÉ left our home, seven officers were forced upon us, one after the other. Among them was a certain Captain Wilcox, who came from Philadelphia when General Howe retreated from that city. He regaled us with tales of a farewell extravaganza given for the retiring general, staged by none other than Captain John André.

"Is he a captain now?" Mother asked.

"Promoted by Lord Howe himself."

Captain Wilcox gossiped how André courted a certain Peggy Shippen, a celebrated young Philadelphia beauty only slightly older than I. "But of course," said Captain Wilcox, "André is a romantic figure and flirts with all the pretty ladies."

Though Mother's eyes were on me, I showed nothing, even as I told myself I cared naught about Captain André.

But by then my life was much engaged. First, I took care of Mother and Father. Secondly, I continued to work for Mr. Gaine at his printing establishment. Mr. Gaine was—or so it seemed—a strong supporter of the

British monarchy, writing and organizing his four-page weekly newspaper accordingly. Even so, I felt obliged to tell him about William. He expressed condolences, but Mr. Gaine was never one to reveal his complete thoughts.

A constant flow of men came into his shop. Some were there to buy books, pamphlets, or medicines. Many were there to leave advertisements, bring news, or hear rumors. Mr. Gaine called these people news-mongers, people who *must* know what is happening before it is published. They therefore knew that in the spring of 1780 the war was going badly for our new country. Charleston, in Carolina, was under siege and believed likely to fall. If it did—so it was thought—the whole South would be lost.

For my part, I felt a boiling fury that there appeared no likelihood that America would win the war and secure its independence. Somebody needed to do something.

Where was Washington?

Where was Arnold?

Who would revenge William's death?

Then I met Robert Townsend and everything changed.

· 32 ·

IT WAS AN evening in May 1780, and I was going home after a day's work upon Mr. Gaine's press. The air was heavy and humid, with alternate moments of sun and squally rain, which is to say, an ordinary New York spring day.

At the press earlier that day, Mr. Gaine had been engaged in conversation with a Mr. Townsend, who was in the shop quite often. Twenty-five years old, Mr. Townsend was in the dry-goods business. I found him dry too. Slight in stature, with an expanse of brow beneath curly hair, he had a large nose—upon which sat small, round eyeglasses—thin lips, and a strong chin. He kept his hair in pigtail fashion and dressed simply, Quaker-style.

Not one to put himself forward, he was given to mild speech and bland emotions. He appeared interested merely in the births, lives, and deaths of citizens and whatever trifling news there was about the war.

That day, as he spoke to Mr. Gaine, they now and again glanced at me, which I took as a hint that I should blank my ears. Yet when I left the shop at the end of the workday, Mr. Townsend stepped out with me.

We proceeded in the same direction, I in front, wanting to get home before the next plout of rain. When a sudden shower slapped down, I scampered for protection 'neath an open stable roof to wait out the weather. Mr. Townsend joined me in the same dry space. We stood side by side, without speaking.

"Forgive me, mistress," he unexpectedly said, "I believe you work in Mr. Gaine's shop."

"I do, sir."

He offered a slight, formal bow. "Robert Townsend. I'm frequently at his shop."

"Yes, sir. I've seen you. My name is Sophia Calderwood."

We watched the dripping rain.

"Unusual occupation for a young lady," he offered. "Printer." A remark I took as meant to fill the time.

"Expenses being what they are, sir," I replied, "my employment aids my family."

Momentarily, he said, "A large family?"

"Father, Mother, and I."

"You are then, so to speak, the family's son."

"My brother died, sir," I blurted, "three years ago."

"I'm exceedingly sorry. A regrettable accident?"

Stung by the casualness of the remark—my thoughts about William were never far—I snapped, "I doubt dying in a foul prison ship should be considered an accident." Embarrassed to have overspoke, I stepped away. "Good evening, sir."

I scurried home. Once there I suppressed my ever-simmering rage about the British, while promising myself I'd give no further thought to Mr. Townsend.

Two days later, however, the man showed up at Mr. Gaine's shop again. As was often the case, gentlemen were there discussing war news—in particular, the Siege of Charlestown. Mr. Townsend ventured no opinion, but, as always, mostly listened. Soon after, he departed.

At my usual hour, I headed for home. Within moments I became aware of footsteps. I looked round. It was Mr. Townsend.

His formal bow. "Forgive me, Miss Calderwood," he said gravely. "Since we exchanged words, I've wanted to speak to you."

"Yes, sir," I said, reminding myself that this time I must keep my tongue better tempered.

"I fear," he said, "when you mentioned the death of your brother, I didn't have the presence of mind to offer my condolences."

"Thank you," I said, and moved on.

He kept in step. "You said he died in one of the prison ships. A rebel soldier?"

"A *patriot* soldier," I said before catching myself.

"Alas," he murmured. "It's said there are thousands languishing in the various prisons in and around the city. The prison hulk the *Jersey* in Wallabout Bay being the worst. And in this heat. Have you heard of Provost Cunningham?"

Merely to hear that loathsome name stressed me. "Forgive me, sir," I snapped. "I don't wish to talk about these matters. Good evening." I hurried on, satisfied that Mr. Townsend did not follow. Still, I was puzzled why he should speak to me at all.

The day following, I was alone in the printer's shop filling composing sticks with lines of advertisements for next Monday's edition of the *Mercury*. Hearing a sound, I turned. There again was Mr. Townsend. "Forgive me, sir. I didn't hear you. May I be of assistance?"

His annoying bow. "I was hoping to speak to Mr. Gaine."

"Was he expecting you?"

"I think not."

"I don't know when he'll arrive, sir. Can I take a message?"

"It will keep. Good morning," he murmured, and turned to go. But upon reaching the door, he paused. "Miss Calderwood, I cannot free my mind of what you said about your unfortunate brother. It must be exceedingly difficult, being a young woman and thereby incapable of taking his place."

"I do wish it were otherwise," I said, my irritation on the rise.

He gazed at me for a moment and then said, "Sometimes, Miss Calderwood, it can be done."

"How, sir?"

A formless hand gesture. "It's the leap year. Women are given leave. Yes, we must speak again." Then, as if plucking something from the air, he abruptly said, "Do you know Mr. Rivington?"

Everyone knew Mr. Rivington. In the fall of 1777, he

had been appointed Printer to the King's Most Excellent Majesty. Given license to publish Wednesday and Saturday, twice the rate as any other paper, he called his newspaper the *Royal Gazette* and supported the British. Though my father detested Rivington's views, he was compelled to do his copy work by way of income. That was my sole connection to Mr. Rivington. Why Mr. Townsend should mention the man, I could not fathom.

Yet after asking me that, Mr. Townsend remained silent, as if trying to come to a decision. In the end he merely said, "My compliments to Mr. Gaine."

With those words, he left.

What are this man's intentions? I kept thinking. *Does he have some meaning? Is he suggesting I should take William's place?* Yes, that was a thought I often had. But how could I, Sophia Calderwood, a refined and educated young woman, do so? Indeed, what might anything I undertook have to do with Mr. Townsend?

Then, when Mr. Gaine came back, the first thing *he* said was "Was Mr. Townsend here? He had an appointment to meet me."

I was sure Mr. Townsend had voiced the opposite. All I said, however, was "He only just left."

"It can't matter," said Mr. Gaine.

But I thought—it *must* matter. No sooner had Mr. Townsend *left* than Mr. Gaine *arrived*—as if they had conspired so that Mr. Townsend might speak to me privately.

Why?

✦ 33 ✦

NEXT MORNING I needed to stop at Mr. Rivington's print shop to deliver editing work done by my father. Mr. Townsend was there. He seemed to be shadowing me! Refusing to even look at him, I delivered Father's work and left. Mr. Townsend followed me onto the street.

"Miss Calderwood," he called. "Are you going to Mr. Gaine?"

"Yes, sir," I said, feeling harassed.

He was silent awhile, then said, "It's not commonly known, but I am Mr. Rivington's business partner."

What has this to do with me? I wondered.

"I'm called a sleeping partner," he went on. "That's to say, we share, without public knowledge, ownership of a coffee house. The Kings Crown. Near Peck's Slip."

When I said nothing, he resumed. "It's a favorite place for British officers."

As if I care about British officers! I stopped and faced him. "Mr. Townsend, I cannot imagine the purpose of your continual chatter. Do you have some purpose?"

He eyed me gravely. A young lady was not supposed

to challenge a man. He even studied the street as if to see if we were being observed.

"Miss Calderwood," he said, "Mr. Gaine speaks of your high intelligence. Your remarkable memory."

"Sir—" I tried to interrupt.

"I've noted the story of your brother," he persisted, "and that you've taken his loss much to heart. During previous conversations, you implied you wished you *could* do something in his place. For his cause. The patriot cause. Is that correct?"

This talk was dangerous.

"Please, sir," I said. "I don't wish to discuss my private thoughts." I stepped away, eager to get to Mr. Gaine's shop.

"But, Miss Calderwood," he called after me, "I might be able to help you achieve your aim."

Without replying, I walked on. But how could I avoid wondering what kind of *help* he was suggesting? I almost wished he had followed me, that he might explain himself. What was he after? Was this dull man offering a courtship? How repelling!

My day at the printing shop proved long. Though I concentrated hard on my duties, Mr. Townsend's words pried upon my thoughts. What aims did he think I had? To be sure, I would have given much to help the patriot cause. Regardless: What could Mr. Townsend offer me in that regard? Or *I* to him?

May I remind you, I was living in a city occupied by the enemy. To act *against* that enemy was to court great hazard. No one knew that better than I did.

At one point during the afternoon, I turned to Mr. Gaine and said, "Mr. Gaine, sir, Mr. Townsend is your close acquaintance. What is your opinion of him?"

Mr. Gaine, after some thought, said, "He is a man whom you can trust."

Trust with what? What game is in play?

❖ 34 ❖

THE DAY FOLLOWING, Mr. Gaine asked me to deliver a small parcel of books. Nothing unusual in that. What made me uneasy was that I was instructed to give them to a British officer, a Sergeant Cook. Moreover, the place for delivery was the coffeehouse near Peck's Slip, the Kings Crown. This, I instantly recalled, was Mr. Rivington's establishment, the one that Mr. Townsend secretly owned with the Tory printer.

When I approached the Kings Crown, parcel in hand, I hesitated. Women were not always welcome in such places. Besides, I could not push aside my conviction that I had been lured here by a plot concocted by Mr. Gaine and Mr. Townsend. I don't mean to suggest I sensed bodily harm. Yet if I had known then what was to be asked of me, I suspect I might not have taken one step within.

The ground floor of the two-story wooden building was a large, open room, illuminated by lamps and candles, which added to the heat of the day. Posts held up the ceiling's oak beams. Tables and Windsor chairs were set about at random. Brown wainscoting lined the walls. On these walls were tacked notices of merchant ship arrivals and departures along with cargos and prices. Official proclamations pertaining to trade were there, along with a gaudy-colored penny-portrait of King George. At the far back of the room was an enclosed area where the coffee maker worked his large copper kettles, cooking the coffee. The drink was served in saucers, distributed by a waiter.

At one table sat three British officers. At another, two. Others sat alone. The British officers were talking loudly. A second group—they seemed to be merchants—kept their voices low.

No one took notice of me. Uncertain, I approached the enclosed area, with its large window overlooking the room. Within, a man tended a fire. The smell of coffee was strong.

"Yes, miss?" said the man when I drew close. "How can I help you?" His face was pox-scarred and sweaty.

"I have a parcel for Sergeant Cook."

The man examined me with his squinty eyes, and then pointed to a soldier sitting alone and reading a newspaper. I approached him.

"Sir?"

He glanced up.

"Mr. Gaine asked me to deliver this to you, sir."

"Ah, yes," he said, and held out his hands. "Thank you. Much obliged."

I handed him the parcel. He took it, set it on the tabletop, and resumed his reading, taking no more note of me.

I stood confused and embarrassed. Was this *all* that was to happen? An *errand*? With a sense of being fooled—and disappointed—I turned and moved toward the door. When I did, a man rose from the table nearest the door. Mr. Townsend.

I halted immediately.

"Miss Calderwood," he said with his customary bow. "I am pleased to meet you."

I glared at him.

"Forgive me," he said, his voice low. "Mr. Gaine suggested that you would be here on his behalf. I won't detain you for a moment."

"Why did you want me to come here?" I demanded.

"I wished you to know this place."

"Why?"

Instead of answering, he asked, "May I walk with you back to Mr. Gaine?"

"Sir, you may have tricked *me* into coming here, but I cannot control what *you* do." I stepped onto the cobblestone street.

As Mr. Townsend kept by my side, I hastened on. He spoke shortly. "Miss Calderwood, did you notice any difference between merchants and soldiers at the Crown?"

"Their dress, obviously," I replied, aware that he was drawing me in. "And the soldiers talk loudly."

"Exactly. Did you hear? They were talking about the fall of Charleston. The British think the end of the war is near."

"They have thought so for years."

"Their thoughts could be of value."

"Not to me, sir."

"But," he said softly, "I'm sure General Washington would like to know what they think."

I halted and faced him with astonishment. "*General Washington?*"

A quick finger to his lips. "Shhh."

I gawked at him. "Mr. Townsend, what are you suggesting?"

"Miss Calderwood," he said, his gaze firmer than I would have given him credit for. "I'm not *suggesting*. I am revealing a fact."

"You mean," I started to say, "you are getting information for—"

A quick hand of caution. "Just say, here too, I am a sleeping partner."

I could have little doubt he was telling me he was a spy! But all I said was "Are Mr. Gaine and Mr. Rivington both in this partnership?"

"One hopes their *public* reputations proclaim otherwise."

I said, "You haven't answered my question, sir."

"It must suffice." He was quiet for a moment, then said, "Miss Calderwood, I know about you, your father, and your brother. Moreover, you have intimated to me that you would like to take some part in our struggle. Your reputation proclaims that you are a patriot, smart, quick, and with a superior memory."

I felt like a stuck pig. "Speak it out, sir," I cried with frustration, though fearful of his answer. "How could I play a part?"

I must have spoken too loudly, for he glanced about, then said, "I think it would be better if we walked. And I beg you. Lower your voice. Let's not draw attention."

We went on without speaking.

In time he said, "With the fall of Charleston, our situation is precarious. Miss Calderwood, you asked, 'How could I play a part in this struggle?' I know of a way."

I whispered, "What would it be?"

His only answer was "I presume you will be at Mr. Gaine's shop tomorrow?"

I nodded.

"Better to talk in private," he said. "Good day, Miss Calderwood." He went off.

* 35 *

THINK ME NOT a bufflehead. I understood Mr. Townsend's meaning. He called himself a "sleeping partner," a sly way of saying "spy." Moreover, the way he referred to General Washington left me in no doubt for whom he was securing information.

That said, I was astonished. I had believed Mr. Townsend the tamest of men. Then I recalled how he listened and did not offer opinions like other men. But he *did* ask many questions. I now understood he lived the proverb "Wise heads have quiet tongues and eager ears."

Yet that he revealed this to *me*, that he chose to connect *me* with what *he* was doing, and seemed to suggest that *I* too could be a spy, was extraordinary. To begin, it was considered base that *anyone* should do a low, dishonorable, deceitful thing as spy. How could I—a fifteen-year-old virtuous girl—act so?

And the danger. *The peril.* More than three years had passed, but it took only an instant for me to recall Nathan Hale's death and Provost Cunningham's words to him, "No Bibles for damned rebel spies." How well I remembered his words to *me*: "Be still, missy, or you'll come to the same fate!"

Most powerfully of all, I recalled William, and his companions, the horrors of the sugarhouse and the *Good Intent*. I had heard that there were women prisoners on the prison ship *Jersey*. Would I risk all that? And yet it was those same appalling facts that reminded me of my profound craving to avenge such crimes.

Thus, it must be said: when I grasped the implication of Mr. Townsend's words, a tremor of exhilaration passed through me. Did I not constantly chide myself about my unfulfilled vow to avenge my brother's death?

Yet what had I *done*? Nothing.

Did I not remind myself of our Declaration and its list of British crimes? Was I not a patriot?

Yet what had I *done*? Nothing.

What of Mother's strong words, that I must find my courage and use it?

Yet what I had *done*? Nothing.

Here, at last, was opportunity.

But—come solutions, come quibbles. What if I were found out? Did I wish to practice such trickery? If caught, could I accept an end to life by hanging? Did I not have a responsibility toward my parents? What if they lost another child—me? Who would care for them in a reduced state and in old age? What if I were unable to do what Mr. Townsend asked? What if I made hash of it all?

Like bees upon the whitest flower, these questions swarmed round me. Of answers, I had none.

✦ 36 ✦

I WALKED HOME along Broadway, my head swirling with these hard thoughts. As if to tease me, the air was soft, almost sweet, but such was my agitated humor, I reminded myself that spring is most unpredictable.

From somewhere I heard music playing. I soon discovered its origins when I went by the Trinity Church ruins. That evening it was aglow with candles and colored paper lanterns, a weekly event. While musicians played and armed soldiers kept mere citizens at bay, British and Hessian officers and their women danced about and *on* the old graves. To my sensibilities, it was an image of what the British were doing to my country. How I despised them.

Then, as I drew closer to home, a new question weighed upon me: Should I tell my parents what I was considering? I had no doubt that they would insist I *not* do what Mr. Townsend requested.

I chose to say nothing. *There*, I chided myself, *I am already deceiving my parents!*

At some point during the evening, our currently

billeted officer, Captain Ponton, arrived. He was a loud, rude man, and I had no fondness for him. Moreover, that night he was somewhat bosky. After idle talk—about how the British would soon trample Americans everywhere—he staggered up to his room. With him gone, my parents took themselves off. Happily, I was left alone with my mind.

I sat there wondering what specifically Mr. Townsend would ask me to do. Would it be hard? Easy? How dangerous? Did I have the courage?

At some point, I heard a soft rapping on our door. Having dozed, I started. Picking up the low-burning candle, I went to the door, eased it open, and peeked out.

A large man was standing on our step, cocked hat pulled down, partly concealing his face. I could see he was not clean, wore a rough jacket, baggy trousers, and muddy boots, and that he was looking at me with puzzlement, as if he had, perhaps, come to the wrong door.

Suddenly, I recognized him. "John Paulding?" I cried. "Is that you?"

I suspect you'll not recall the name. Mr. Paulding was William's friend, the one who urged him to join the army just before the battle in Brooklyn. The last time I'd seen him was when the two marched off together.

"And you are—?"

"Sophia Calderwood."

"Miss Calderwood! Forgive me. You've quite grown."

I reached to draw him inside.

He held back. "Is it safe to come in?"

"We have a British officer forced upon us," I said.

He pulled away. "Can we go round back?" he asked.

I nodded. As he retreated, I followed him, candle in hand. I found him sitting on the ground. I blew the candle out, knelt by his side, and poured out questions. "Where have you come from? Where have you been? Why did you come?"

He told me that ever since that battle in Brooklyn he'd been mostly with Washington's army, moving up and down the country. His stories were amazing and affecting. He had seen and done much.

Only recently he'd been posted to Westchester County—his native area—where he had been ordered to patrol what was called the "neutral country." This was the area just north of Manhattan under the control of neither patriot nor Tory. His task was to watch for pillaging Tories—called "cowboys"—and prowling redcoats.

Being close to the city, he'd come to visit his intended wife—Miss Sarah Teed—whom he had not seen in many months. He was also determined to pay his respects to my parents. "I'd heard of William's death some while ago," he said. "I've long wished to come, but I haven't been able. I'm awful sorry." So it was that this night, knowing officers would be distracted by the Trinity dance, he slipped across the lines and made his way.

"Thank you," I said. "You were ever the good friend. Was it dangerous to come?"

"The neutral area is always infested with thieves, spies, as well as enemy soldiers. But, Miss Calderwood,

I'm not sure I know what danger is anymore. Tell me about William. Do you blame me for getting him to enlist?"

"You were not the only one to urge him. And we were proud of him." I related to Mr. Paulding all that happened to cause his death.

Though he knew about the sugarhouse and prison ships, William's story made him angry. "You must," he said, "give your parents my condolences."

He asked me about myself, but I spoke only about my work with Mr. Gaine, nothing about Mr. Townsend's offer.

He told me he needed to leave the city quickly, it being risky for him to stay. "They would make short work of me if I were to be caught. But from this time forward, Miss Calderwood," he added earnestly, "I beg you, consider me your brother. If ever you need anything, leave word for me at the place called Tarrytown."

Though I could not imagine doing such a thing, I was touched. I thanked Mr. Paulding with all my heart. He in turn gave me a quick, brotherly embrace and slipped into the night.

Certain I would not see him again, I went to the common room and gave myself to my decision about Mr. Townsend.

I do not mean to claim that Mr. Paulding's coming that night caused me to make up my mind. No more than did seeing those officers dance upon the sacred graves at Trinity Church. Or Captain Ponton's crude and tipsy remarks. Only that they proved very timely. Perhaps, as it's said, coincidences are God's small messages.

Surely, if Mr. Paulding could expose himself to so much danger on behalf of our country, if William could give his life, if Nathan Hale could give his, if I must witness British officers dance upon our graves, how dare *I* do nothing? Need I remind you I had reason and motive enough? All these things gave blood to my heart.

Thus, I made up my mind. I would join Robert Townsend. I would become a spy.

❖ 37 ❖

NEXT MORNING I went off to Hanover Square. For most of the day I worked setting lines of advertising type. Dull work indeed, and tedium agitates the soul. My mind spun about the questions I would pose to Mr. Townsend.

It was late afternoon when he appeared. When he came in, he did not even look at me, but conversed with Mr. Gaine about small matters. Perhaps Mr. Townsend had changed *his* mind. Part of me wished he had.

At length, however, Mr. Townsend turned to me. Bowed. "Miss Calderwood, good afternoon."

Curtsy. "Good afternoon, sir."

"Might you wish a word with me?"

Mr. Gaine shifted round so deliberately, I was sure he understood what was afoot.

"Yes, sir," I replied.

Mr. Gaine removed his leather apron and said, "Forgive me, Mr. Townsend. I've got me a small errand. Miss Calderwood, be so good as to look after."

"Yes, sir," I replied, certain he did not wish to hear my conversation with Mr. Townsend. Indeed, within moments that gentleman turned to me and said, "Miss Calderwood, have you come to a decision?"

I said, "I wish to help."

"Bravo."

"But, Mr. Townsend," I said in haste, "I first need to know how you intend to make use of me."

"There is a house servant position available in the British headquarters at number one Broadway. I've been asked to find a young woman to take on the chores there."

"But how could my being a house servant help?"

"Within such a place there must be much unguarded talk. Papers left about. The like. All you need do is look and listen. An opportunity not to be missed."

"Mr. Townsend—"

"Anything you believe is significant you shall convey to me. No more. No less."

"Won't they discover me?"

"The world being what it is, Miss Calderwood, your being a girl shall mask your true occupation."

Nothing he said could have excited me more. "Can you really place me in the position?"

"I'm on good terms with someone in the household. Not that they know me—as you do. So, yes."

No sooner confronted with reality than I felt queasy. I turned my back on him and thought of ways to wiggle free. "One problem, sir. My parents depend upon my wages."

"Whatever you earn here, Miss Calderwood, you will receive the same amount. I will answer for it."

He would say no more but waited. As for me, I could think of no other rational objections to Mr. Townsend's offer, save fright, which I was not prepared to admit.

"When would I begin?"

"Tomorrow."

"Tomorrow!"

"Our need for information is urgent. We don't wish to lose any opportunity."

"Mr. Townsend," I abruptly asked. "How did you come to this employment?"

"Did you ever hear of Nathan Hale?"

Startled, I could only stare.

"When Hale died, General Washington established a scheme of spies. Mr. Paine's words recruited me." Leaving me to assume the rest, Mr. Townsend asked, "Are you still willing?"

I said, "How secret shall this be?"

"Only you, Miss Calderwood, and I shall know."

"But Mr. Gaine—"

He brushed the question aside with a wave of his hand. "Now, then," he hurried on, "tomorrow morning at eight o'clock you shall meet me outside the Archibald Kennedy house—number one Broadway."

Feeling rushed, I found another excuse. "But if I *do* discover something, how can I inform you?"

"You shall leave notes for me—under the name Culper—at the Kings Crown. That's why I wished you to see it. Have you other questions?"

I could think of none.

"Then we agree?"

I think I nodded. Oh, fateful nod!

It was then he added, "I must give one warning. This is a dangerous thing I—and now you—will be doing. To be found out could be fatal. It's best to be skittish. From time to time, I might even find it best to withdraw. That means there may be times you will be without me."

"And if I am?"

"You will need to make decisions on your own. Can you do that?"

What could I say other than "I think so"?

"Then, till tomorrow." That said, Mr. Townsend left me.

At home that night my talk was so small that Mother wanted to know if I was ill. I assured her I was fine.

Indeed, out of a sense of obligation—I might be taken and held without their knowing—I finally blurted out what I was about to do. As I expected, my parents were appalled. Urged me not to. Spoke of it as folly. Of danger. As my parents, they ordered me not to.

Their opposition became my strength. To every argument, fear, and threat, my only answer was "I'm doing it for William. His comrades." I would not be turned.

Not as strong as I, they eventually gave up.

Oh, you who would prefer weak parents. Think again!

I spent a tossing night, wondering about all that might happen. How would I comport myself? Was I capable of deception? Would I know what information was of value? What way would I convey that information to Mr. Townsend? Why use a false name—Culper—for messages? He hinted he might have to withdraw for a while. Would I—if necessary—be able to deal alone?

Would Mr. Townsend really give the information I provided to General Washington? How would he do so?

I had no answers to such questions.

Moreover, it came to me that the oft-used symbol for Great Britain was a lion, and that on the morrow, I was going to place myself in the beast's great, sharp-toothed jaws.

☀ 38 ☀

I AWOKE BEFORE I needed to. I breakfasted and hurried to market for Mother. Happily, I had no papers to deliver for Father. Without further words to my stony-faced parents, I walked to number one Broadway.

The city knew no grander building than the one known as the Archibald Kennedy house. A large two-story—plus attic—brick building, it was almost sixty feet wide at the street. On each of the two main floors were four big windows, all with shutters. The entryway was a massive white door reached by four stone steps, the door bracketed with stately wooden and fluted columns. The closer I came to this commanding structure, the more my resolution shrank. Did I really wish to commit myself to such an outrageous act—to be a spy?

When I stood before the building and saw two tall British guards—one on each side of the front door, standing at fierce attention, bayoneted muskets in hand—I struggled to maintain my resolve. Even as I observed it all, other soldiers—they appeared to be officers—were entering and leaving the house.

"Miss Calderwood."

Startled, I looked around. It was Mr. Townsend.

"We need to go round the back," he said quietly.

Led by him, I went down an alley on the north side of the building. At the rear was a low door—the servants' entrance, but guarded as out front, by two soldiers.

Mr. Townsend approached them. One of the soldiers seemed to recognize him. "We're here to see Mrs. Benjamin."

"Very good, Mr. Townsend." The soldier saluted Mr. Townsend but took no notice of me. It made me recall Mr. Townsend's remark that "Your being a girl shall mask your true occupation." Now "folly," not "occupation," seemed a better word.

The other solider opened the door for us.

We stepped down into a spacious kitchen with an immense hearth and stone floor, as well as tables, cabinets, and large basins. On one wall, bright copper pots were shelved in orderly fashion. Others hung from the ceiling. Barrels stood about, containing I knew not what. On the massive central table, mounds of vegetables, a large fish, a side of beef, plus loaves of bread. Considering the city's shortage of food, it was astonishing to see such abundance. It filled me with resentment and stiffened my resolve.

Three women were hard at work preparing food. Two were young, and the third was a large, elder woman, who turned to greet us.

"Ah, Mr. Townsend. Good day."

"Mrs. Benjamin, this is the girl I spoke to you about."

I curtsyed as the woman eyed me up and down.

"Very well," said Mrs. Benjamin. "We can try her. Miss, if you would sit there, I'll send for Mrs. Ticknor. She's chief housekeeper. She'll inform you of your duties. Mr. Townsend," she said, "much obliged."

To her he said, "I'll send that cloth you requested to your home." To me he *said* nothing but gave me his customary brief bow and departed.

I took the chair where I'd been directed, and waited. One of the younger women left the room, presumably to fetch that Mrs. Ticknor. Since Mrs. Benjamin and the other young woman paid no further notice of me, I sat there trying to take in as much as I could, while pondering the notion that in exchange for a bolt of cloth, I had been engaged as a spy.

I was still sitting there waiting when into the room stepped John André.

❖ 39 ❖

MY HEART LURCHED. My throat tightened. I could hardly breathe. All I did was gawk at him.

As for John André, he went right to Mrs. Benjamin and spoke about some special guests to be at that night's dinner with General Clinton. A discussion of the menu ensued. At one point he casually glanced round the room and rested his eyes on me.

Did he recognize me? I saw not so much as a glimmer of notice in his eyes. No, he knew me not, no more than had John Paulding. Once a girl, now a woman. What better disguise! Next instant he turned away, finished talking, then left. The kitchen resumed what it had been doing before.

"Mrs. Benjamin," I said when I could carry on with normal breathing, "that officer who was just here, who is he?"

"Major André? He's General Henry Clinton's chief of staff. Just back from Charleston. Next to His Excellency, the general, he's the most powerful man here."

"Is he a major, then?"

"And soon to be promoted higher, they say."

"What are his duties?"

"Lord. What doesn't he do? Schedules the general's appointments and sees everyone who comes. Receives and answers the general's letters. Approves sick leave. Writes reports for the general. In all of General Clinton decisions, he has a part. And, so it's said, he's scout-master."

"Scoutmaster?"

"You know: the word they use for the one in charge of intelligence. Spies and the like. I daresay our army has a host of them. And the rebels, I suppose, have theirs. Major André is not only in charge of our spies, he's supposed to catch the rebel ones."

✦ 40 ✦

JUST BEFORE, MY heart had been beating wildly. Now I truly believed it had stopped altogether.

"Very well, then," Mrs. Benjamin went on without noticing my reaction. "What name do you wish to be called?"

Who *thinks* about one's choice of name? But somehow I managed to find tongue enough to give my mother's name. "Molly," I managed to say. "Molly Saville."

Mrs. Ticknor arrived in the kitchen. She was a small, plump, red-faced middle-aged woman, bursting with much forcibility. Despite her size, the woman attended to her duties like a barn swallow, forever swooping here, there, and everywhere. In her charge were nine housemaids, first and second floor, of which I was the newest.

"Never forget," she prattled rapidly as she gave me a tour, "this house is the most important in the city and, I daresay, in the country. His Excellency General Henry Clinton insists that things be done to perfection."

From floor to ceiling, wealth and fashion gilded every inch of the headquarters. The outsized rooms all had fireplaces with marble mantels, stylish chairs with tapestry backings and cushions, as well as graceful tables on thick rugs. Crystal chandeliers—loaded with bayberry candles—dangled from ceilings. Upon the walls hung portraits of bewigged and bemetaled military men who gazed condescendingly down from their perches.

The top floor housed General Clinton's living quarters. I was instructed that I was a "first-floor girl, and not to go where I was not asked." During my time there, I generally did not know the general was about unless I heard him playing his violin in his private quarters.

The first-floor up-front rooms were the dining room and parlor. The parlor served as a waiting room for those who came to call upon the general. Indeed, there were crowds of such visitors—officers, government men, and merchants—morning, noon, and night. Dinners were as elaborate as they were late.

My tasks, as Mrs. Ticknor unfolded them, appeared endless: polishing windows, floors, and door locks. Dusting picture frames, mantels, desks, and chairs. I was to serve food, take dishes away, and when called upon, wash linen, napkins, and the like. In short, I must do whatever I was told. Further, I was to be in the house no later than six in the morning and would be released only in the evenings, until I was no longer needed.

On that first floor, in the back, was the commander in chief's office. Directly across the hallway, with special access, was John André's place of work. Mrs. Ticknor stopped before the door and announced, "I need to show you Major André's office. Cleaning it will be a key part of your duties."

Alarm enveloped me. *What if he is there? What if this time he recognizes me?*

All the same, I wished to see it, the more so when Mrs. Ticknor, hand on the doorknob, spoke with reverence. "You must pay attention to the major. He's risen swiftly, and will go far. Everyone acknowledges he's that rarity, a favorite of General Clinton. The two confer about *everything*. Indeed, they say nothing happens in this house to which the major is not a party." She lowered her voice: "The power behind the throne.

"But for all his importance," she went on, "the major is courteous and, while firm, doesn't seek fault. His friendly and ungrudging ways have made him a favorite of the staff. We all dearly love him. I'm sure you will too."

Why did that give me a pinch of pain?

She knocked—my heart was knocking too—and upon receiving no answer, opened the door.

I was thankful—or was I disappointed?—the room was deserted. I examined it. There was a large table in the center of his room—a chair behind it, two chairs before. Upon the table were many papers. A few lay spread about, but most were in neat stacks. Writing quills stuck up from a wide mouthed jar next to an inkwell and a box of blotting sand. On one wall, a portrait of someone in an elegant uniform. Mostly, however, the walls bore pinned-up maps, more than I had ever seen. As for what places they represented, I could not say.

Like every other room in the house, it had a large fireplace, but this being summer, no fire was laid. I did note that André's flute lay upon the mantel. Recalling how he used to play for me, it was impossible not to have emotioned thoughts. I did my first dusting while denying them away.

"He's been working hard of late," Mrs. Ticknor went on, her voice ripe with respect. "He arrives in his office before the general and stays much later. It shall be your responsibility to get here in the morning each day, before he does, to tidy."

Mrs. Ticknor said no more but, putting a dust cloth in my hand, set me to polishing brass fixtures in the dining room.

As I went about my tasks that first day, I tried to speculate what kind of information might be in those papers I had seen on Major André's desk. If this was "the most important house in the city" and "nothing happens in this house to which the major is not a party," his office must contain a trunk of useful intelligence. It was my task to unpack those things, *not* to engage with the major.

41

MY FIRST WEEK of work, though arduous, proved typical. Chores were endless, and of small interest. I arrived early and left late, worn out. That said, my fear of discovery subsided, because the only ones who paid any attention to me were my sister cleaners and Mrs. Ticknor.

Indeed, it was rare for me to labor alone. That said, the women I worked with were quite companionable. While we toiled, there were moments of casual chatter and gossip, which I was interested to hear. Much talk was about various officers being sent off, who was dashing, who disgraced, who praised, and the like. Indeed, among the girls there was some competition as to who could learn—and share—the most. The wages of drudgery is gossip.

The common view about the war was that it could not last long, that American fortunes were much diminished, that of the British Army ascending. But then, most of the women were passionate loyalists. Did they care that the king imposed taxes on us without consent or cut off our trade from the world? Think of dying prisoners? Not a jot! I would have loved to argue reason into them but dared not. Indeed, I found their loyalist chat of use.

Of John André, one of them confided, "With all his open charm, there is much that is closed in him."

Another passing comment: that Major André, since the capture of Charleston (in the Carolinas), had been focused on *something* that required lengthy conferences with General Clinton. The gossip was that a grand military action—"some bold stroke"—was under review. As someone said, "Hopefully, it will bring a quick end to the war."

You may well perceive my keen desire to know what that *bold stroke* might be.

I saw John André regularly, and absolutely, he did not recognize me. He was courteous and kind to me but took no notice in any way. His smiles were bestowed on everyone. His regard was such that I might as well have been invisible.

On my part, I found him not so different from three years previous. His uniform was more elaborate—as befitted his higher rank—while his olive-hued skin, dark eyes, and black hair set him off to good advantage. His face still gave every suggestion of honest openness. Though I knew he was a soldier and had seen coarse times, I could have believed the word "charming" had been invented for him. Hardly a wonder that he was a favorite.

But what did I *feel* about him? Each time I saw him, I asked myself that question. Though I searched my heart for answers, I was convinced I found no affixedness. Instead, I insisted that the flush of sensibility I felt whenever I saw him was merely fear of discovery. I had but to think that he could have saved William, and all the horrors of my brother's death rose before me. To that dreadfulness what had André said? "I must not let the slightest hint of irregularity brush against my honor as a British officer."

His honor. *My* dear William!

So you may be sure, I insisted that John André was the enemy. I *must* hate him.

And yet I was dimly aware of this contradiction: I wished him to notice me, while aware that if he did, it might well prove fatal.

❖ 42 ❖

ON MY SECOND day of work I found myself—as would be the case almost every day—in Major André's office, cleaning with another housemaid. Once there, I seized the opportunity to tidy his desk that I might read anything that lay there.

All too quickly, I realized that while I could read some papers, I had access only to the top-most sheets unless I shifted them, which I was loath to do. Moreover, since my opportunities were but fleeting, it was fortunate that I could read as fast as I could.

Upon that first occasion, I discovered nothing I thought would be of interest to Mr. Townsend. I could only trust there would be other opportunities.

There did prove one perplexing difficulty. There were *many* papers on the major's desk. Which ones were written in André's hand, and which were not, I could not readily determine.

However, that night when I got home, I found a way to solve that problem: the poem John André had written to me. I had it still in a tin box, hidden away along with the blue ribbon. Once the poem was retrieved, I studied it anew.

> *No matter how young the flower*
> *Which has yet to burst to bloom,*
> *The time will come, its finest hour*
> *When she'll be prettiest in my room.*

While I learned his singular hand, I could not help but notice this quirk of fate: looking and learning the hand he used to *win* me was my means of causing him to *lose*. Or so I hoped.

43

IN THE DAYS that followed, I had much access to John André's desk, but discovered nothing. Then, on the eighth day of June, a Reverend Jonathan Odell called upon the major.

I learned Mr. Odell's name because the girl with whom I was working enjoyed telling me—in regular hearsay fashion—that Mr. Odell had been a British officer before going into the Church of England. "He's been a steady visitor of late," she confided. "Meeting with Major André."

Since John André had once taken pains to tell me he had no special interest in matters of religion, I found this curious. "Does Reverend Odell," I asked, "come on church or military matters?"

"I can't say," she confided. "Just seems an important friend. Whenever he comes, the major puts all business aside, brings Mr. Odell within his office, and locks the door."

"What do you think their dealings are about?"

"I'm sure I don't know. Maybe the major is going into the church." Her giggle assured me it was not likely.

But though my curiosity heightened, I was perplexed as to how I might learn more.

However, two days after Mr. Odell had called at the Kennedy house, I was again cleaning Major André's desk when I glimpsed a paper with the heading "Mr. Moore's Memoranda." What followed was a list:

> *French fleet is on way*
> *Attack on Quebec*
> *West Point is under strength*
> *Hudson's River chain easily smashed*
> *Rocky Hill redoubt weak*
> *Requests £10,000*

Of course, the word "attack" caught my attention, with a sense that this *must* be military in nature. So at last—*something* of interest. And the handwriting was definitely André's.

I studied the list, trying to make sense of what I saw. Though I knew Quebec was a city in Canada, I was ignorant about where or what was West Point. The same for Rocky Hill. Nor did I know what a "redoubt" was. As for "Mr. Moore," the name meant nothing to me.

Believing, however, that the memoranda would be of some interest to Mr. Townsend, I committed as much of the page to my memory as I could.

I also stole a moment to gaze upon the maps that were set upon the wall. They were many, large, and complex. In my brief study, I could not locate a West Point.

That night, when I came home, I wrote down all I

could recall of that memorandum. The following morning I rose early and took a sealed note—inscribed to "Culper"—and went to the Kings Crown. As I expected, it was too early for anyone to be there, but I slipped the paper under the door.

As I walked away, I allowed myself to think, *I am learning John André's secrets.*

It gave me pleasure.

❖ 44 ❖

THE NEXT DAY'S work at the Kennedy house passed without incident. I did some cleaning in Major André's room but discovered only that the memoranda I'd previously seen was gone. Perhaps, I told myself, with disappointment, it meant nothing.

By the time I was told I might go home, it was evening. Like most July nights, it was warm and humid, and I was looking forward to a cooling rest. As I passed up Broadway, however, Mr. Townsend had silently fallen into step by my side.

He offered no greeting, but, speaking in a low voice, said, "Was there any more to that memorandum than you gave me?"

"No, sir. Was it special?"

"Do you have any idea who Mr. Moore is?"

"None. What is West Point?"

"A vital American fort. But it's urgent that you find out who is Mr. Moore."

I said, "Do you know a Mr. Jonathan Odell?"

"An obnoxious Tory churchman. What of him?"

"He visits Major André."

Mr. Townsend merely muttered, "Hmmm."

I said, "Do you wish me—" But when I turned to complete the question, Mr. Townsend was already walking away from me.

I thought, if *he* was so cautious, what should that tell me to do about *my* spying?

A few days later, I was again in André's office, where on his desk I found yet another note in his own hand, which was headed "Mr. Moore." I immediately read it.

French not going to Quebec. Rhode Island. Expects to get command of West Point. Americans sick of war. Wish to be on former footing.

The words, in themselves, made little sense to me. *Who is expected to command West Point? Who wishes to be on former footing?* And indeed, *What footing is that?* Beyond all else, *Who is Mr. Moore?*

As before, I committed the words to memory. When I finally reached home that night, I wrote them out that I might pass the information to "Culper."

I also asked Father if he knew where West Point was.

"I believe it's up along Hudson's River, perhaps some fifty miles beyond Manhattan. On the western shore."

"Who controls it?"

"I believe we do." By *we*, he meant Americans.

"Is it vital?"

"I'm no military strategist, but I would think that if we lost it, New England would be lost. With so much of the South occupied by the British, to lose New England is as much to say *all* might be lost."

"What is a 'redoubt'?"

"A small, detached fortification," he said. "Is all this part of your new, shall I say, occupation?"

I said nothing.

"I suppose you can't tell me more," he said.

To which I said, "Have you ever heard of a Mr. Moore?"

"Never."

Early next morning, I left a note for "Culper" at the Kings Crown. It contained what I had newly learned. For the first time I took pains to look about to make sure I was not being observed.

Later that day, a curious incident. My companion and I were dusting John André's office, including his mantel, and thus the flute. I could not refrain from looking at it, or refrain from thinking how the lieutenant once played for me.

Even as I had that thought, John André entered the room.

"Good morning," he said.

My companion and I curtsied.

Looking at me, he smiled and said to me, "Do you know what that instrument is?"

"A flute, sir?"

"Good for you." Next moment he picked it up and began to play, only to soon stop. As he replaced it on the mantel, he said, "That was from happier days. Well, I must work. Ladies . . ." He gestured to the door.

My companion and I left. As the door shut behind us, she gave me a nudge. "He likes you." She giggled.

I made no response to her but only felt anger—*How could he have forgotten me?* But a new thought quickly tumbled forward: *I have fooled him!* That realization gave me something I had never experienced before—a sense of power.

The same evening when I was coming home along Broadway, Mr. Townsend passed me without stopping. As he went by, he said, "You *must* find out about Mr. Moore."

"Sir!" But he was gone.

July the fourteenth proved an extraordinary day.

In the morning I had been asked as usual, along with another housemaid, to clean André's office. When we arrived, the major was not there. As it happened, while we were still at work, he again walked in.

I, along with my companion, immediately curtsied, bade him a "Good morning, sir," and took steps to leave.

"No, no," he called. "I've only this letter to copy. But I must have the office ready for a visitor. Go on with your work."

That we did, while he sat down at his table, paper before him. Quill in hand, he commenced to write.

He was still writing when an officer opened the side door—which led to General Clinton's office—poked his head in, and said, "Sir, General Clinton wishes to see you directly."

André put his pen down and went out of the room, shutting the door behind him. The moment he was gone I recalled Mr. Townsend's words "You must find out about Mr. Moore."

With rash impulsiveness, I went to André's desk and read what he had written: it was addressed to Mr. Moore. The part I could read said,

> *HESH is much obliged to you for the useful Intelligence you have transmitted him. It corresponds with other information and gives him full conviction of your desire to assist him. He had hoped to communicate with you in a very satisfactory manner but is disappointed. His Excellency hopes you still keep in view the project of essentially cooperating with him. He thinks having the command of W. Point would afford*

That was all André had written before quitting his desk. Even as I reread it, struggling to commit it to my memory, I heard the squeak of the doorknob. I scurried away.

André reappeared. Unaware of what I'd done, he sat down and resumed writing. When he finished, he blotted the paper with sand, gathered up what he had written, and went back out that side door, presumably to meet with Sir Henry again.

As soon as he left the room, my companion burst into giggles. "You read what he was writing, didn't you? What did it say? I suppose you can read."

Realizing I had acted recklessly—I could feel myself blushing—I nonetheless had wits to say, "He was refusing to grant someone a leave to visit his intended wife and was explaining why."

To my relief the girl made a silly laugh but seemed satisfied.

As the day wore on, I kept turning over in my head what I had read so as to keep it fresh in my memory. At the same time, I continued to wonder who "HESH" was. And West Point was mentioned again. The words implied "Mr. Moore" would have *command* of West Point. What was meant by "cooperating"?

Midafternoon, it came to me: "HESH," meant *H*is *E*xcellency *S*ir *H*enry. And "cooperating" might mean "working with."

I did recall my father's words that if America lost West Point, New England could be lost, and thereby the whole war. And that day the Reverend Odell visited again with André. Were there connections to all this?

That evening, when I got home, the first thing I did was write down as much as I could recall of André's letter. The following morning, as before, I slipped a message under the door of the Kings Crown, saying that I must speak with "Culper." I was satisfied then that the next evening, as I was going home, Mr. Townsend fell in with me.

I told him what I had read.

He said, "To whom was that letter written?"

"That *Mr. Moore.*"

"I have searched," he said with authority. "There is no Moore in the British command. Is the man mentioned at the headquarters?"

"Not that I have heard."

"I suspect it is a false name," he suggested. "You must find out who he really is. It's vital."

We walked farther on, neither of us talking, until he said, "Miss Calderwood, I fear I may have to absent myself for a while."

I halted. "Why?"

"Keep walking. I am not positive, but I may be suspected. You know I cannot take many risks. Though such suspicion has occurred before and proved an empty threat, it will be necessary for me to withdraw for a while."

I was taken aback. "What do you mean, withdraw?"

"My father conducts a business at Oyster Bay. I shall remove there for a time."

"How long?" I said.

"I can't say."

"Is it far?"

"The north shore of Long Island."

"What should I do if I learn some information about Mr. Moore?"

"I'll try to find a way for you to communicate with me."

"Mr. Townsend," I said, "forgive me. But the information I give to you, you once told me it went to General Washington. Do you give it to him yourself? Could I do that?"

He shook his head. "I send it to Connecticut, to a Major Tallmadge, who—" He cut himself short. "Forgive me. I—I should not speak of him," he said with a stammer of embarrassment. "Blot that name from your memory."

"But, Mr. Townsend—"

He had already stepped away.

I watched him go. Insofar as he had given me *no* means of contacting *him*—save his fleeting, forgettable mention of this Tallmadge, I felt quite alone. Of course, telling me *not* to remember caused me to do the opposite. *Tallmadge.* I would remember that name.

❖ 45 ❖

SOME DAYS LATER, in the morning, I was cleaning the vestibule at the Kennedy house when Major André and two other officers passed by me. Talking loudly, they said they'd been given leave to cross the river to Brooklyn, where, that day, horse races were being held. André was in high spirits. It reminded me of the day I walked out with him—full of joy, which utterly evaporated when I saw William as prisoner. My determination to revenge him was recalled. Perhaps that is why I did what I did.

Going to the races: no doubt it was because General Clinton had gone north to Beekman Mansion, where he sometimes stayed. Things were more relaxed at headquarters when the general was at Beekman. In short, we cleaning girls would be left more alone than usual.

As it happened, during the morning, when another girl and I were in Major André's office, there came a knock on the door. Since my companion was closest to the door—I was mopping a corner of the room—she went and opened it. Standing there, letter in hand, was the Reverend Odell.

He held up a sealed letter. "It is of considerable consequence that this letter reach Major André. Would you be so good as to place it on his desk?"

"Of course, sir." My companion took the letter, and when Mr. Odell retired, she shut the door, brought it to the desk, put it down, and resumed her work.

My curiosity was much sparked. As soon as I had an opportunity, I drew close to the desk and glanced at the letter. It was addressed to a "Mr. Anderson."

I gazed at it: *If it is for Major André, who then is Mr. Anderson?*

As I worked about the room, I could not get the letter out of my mind. Wanting much to read it, and certain that André was gone for the day—as was General Clinton—I devised a crude stratagem.

When our cleaning was done, and just as we were stepping out of the room, the door half closed, I said, "I forgot my mop."

I slipped back into the room and picked up the mop where I had deliberately left it near the desk. In almost the same movement, I snatched up the Odell letter and placed it in my apron pocket. Only then did I leave the room.

My companion took no notice.

It was one thing to have the letter. Quite another to read it. Moreover, now that I possessed it, I was aware of the extreme danger in which I had placed myself. Every time someone took any note of me, it was, I was sure, discovery.

What if Major André appeared and asked for it?

What if General Clinton asked?

What if Mr. Odell did as much?

I trembled.

As the day wore on, and I could find no way to read the letter in private, the gross stupidity of what I'd done grew upon me. I had a mind to destroy it. Burn it. But there proved no opportunity. Over time, no letter in a pocket ever weighed more.

Hours passed and I had yet to read or destroy the letter. As more time went by, I grew convinced I must lay it back on the desk. But though people talk of the difficulty of *stealing* something, it is perhaps even harder to *restore* a thing with equal success.

During the afternoon, Mrs. Ticknor told me, along with two other housemaids, to clean the central stairway. Seeing my chance, I took the lead, going up the steps ahead of the others.

Crouched down, back to my companions, I plucked the letter from my pocket, only to realize that my day's movements had broken the wax seal. Fumbling, I opened the letter.

The first thing I noted was the signature at the end, which was "Moore." It other words, it was a letter *from* Mr. Moore.

There was an opening address, and then it read:

I addressed a letter to you expressing my sentiments and expectations, viz, that the following preliminaries be settled previous to cooperating. First, that S Henry secure to me my property, valued at ten thousand

pounds sterling, to be paid to me or my heirs in case of
loss; and as soon as that shall happen, hundred pounds
per annum to be secured to me for life, in lieu of the
pay and emoluments I give up, for my services as they
shall deserve if I point out a plan of cooperation by
which SH shall possess himself of West Point—

I had to read that phrase again and again.

by which SH shall possess himself of West Point—

I suddenly understood: this was a plan to give over
West Point to Sir Henry.

Even as I was reading, I heard a sound behind. I
glanced around and saw Sir Henry himself, back from
his journey north, coming up the steps.

❖ 46 ❖

PANIC-STRUCK, I shoved the letter into my pocket and, head bowed, applied myself desperately to my cleaning task. Next moment the general passed me, going up to his private rooms. He paid no mind to me. Probably he did not even notice me—a girl at her menial work.

Though I wished urgently to reread what I had read—as well as to consider the rest—I was too unsettled.

Rather, I concentrated on my cleaning with but one thought: I *must* replace the letter. Yet there was another thing to do first. Searching out a lit candle, I held the broken seal to the heat and fused it mostly as it was. Then, at the first opportunity, I crept back to Major André's office, forced myself to dart in, and flung the letter on the desk. I escaped even faster, heart pounding like a baby bird's. I spent the remainder of the day in clutching tension that I would be undone. *I must leave this place*, I thought.

But simultaneously I went, so to speak, in an opposite direction; that is, I went over and over what I'd read. For I was perfectly convinced that Mr. Moore—whoever he was—was planning to find a way to have

General Henry Clinton take *possession* of West Point. From what I knew—my father's words seconded by Mr. Townsend—such an event would be an utter catastrophe for the patriot cause.

Nevertheless, there remained that vital unanswered question: *Who* was Mr. Moore? No patriot, of that I could be certain. Further, Mr. Townsend had suggested "Moore" was not a real name, that "Moore" was a fabrication, even as I called myself "Molly Saville."

Was Mr. Odell Mr. Moore? That could hardly be the case. He and André met at headquarters. No need for letters. Odell, I sensed, was merely the *deliverer* of Mr. Moore's letters.

But since West Point was in the hands of Americans, it implied that some *American* was conspiring to deliver the fort to the British. A horrible thought to be sure, and one that made the unmasking of "Moore" desperately urgent.

As I thought about what I *did* know, I supposed the best way of finding out the identity of "Moore" would be to learn who was in command of West Point. But how was I—in British New York—to gain such information? I could hardly ask André. I was sure none of the cleaning girls would know. I was not on speaking terms with any other officer. Just to ask such a question might raise suspicions of me.

But I must tell Mr. Townsend of my discovery. He, however, was gone.

I spent an agitated night trying to decide what to do. During my sleepless hours, I culled the idea that Mr.

Gaine and Mr. Rivington—both of whom, I was convinced, knew what Mr. Townsend was secretly doing *and* were aware of my connection—could help me get a message to him. I decided to go to their printing shops in the morning.

That is what I did.

Mr. Rivington's shop was closest, and I so much wanted him to be there. Indeed he was, dressed fine and bewigged, as was his fashion.

He greeted me, however, guardedly.

"Yes, Miss Calderwood, are you asking for work for your father?"

"I'm trying to locate Mr. Townsend."

"I beg your pardon. I've no knowledge where that gentleman resides."

"He said Oyster Bay."

"Then you know far more than I. Forgive me, Miss Calderwood, I've work to do." In haste, he turned away as if to avoid any other queries—or so I concluded.

I thought of telling Mr. Rivington that I was aware of his business association with Mr. Townsend, but considered it imprudent.

The thought came: Had something happened to Mr. Townsend that compelled Mr. Rivington to avoid any dealings with him?

I was increasingly troubled.

I hastened on to Mr. Gaine. He too was at work. I asked him if *he* knew how to reach Mr. Townsend. He frowned, and though no one else was in his shop, he took me into a corner. In a low voice he said, "I believe

Mr. Townsend is, of necessity, concealed. Many are these days. The British are actively searching. But, Miss Calderwood, I beg you not to think *I* have any notion where he is." He spoke the word "beg" as if pleading.

Clearly, the message was I must be equally cautious.

There I was, merely a girl, but one who had uncovered a huge secret. One of the greatest importance. But my excitement over my discovery was turning into terror. How could I be expected to know what to do? I had to tell someone who could act. Frustrated, scared, I went off to the Kennedy house. I was, moreover, increasingly angry with Mr. Townsend for having abandoned me. He might be safely hidden, but I was trapped in the lion's den with a great secret in my hands.

And though I had discovered much, there was one more vital fact I did not know: Who was Mr. Moore?

❖ 47 ❖

THOUGH I WISHED it otherwise, in the following days Mr. Townsend did not appear.

I took it upon myself—when I had the opportunity—to study the maps in André's office and search out West Point. Father had said it lay upon the western shore of Hudson's River, some fifty miles north of the city. That enabled me to locate it on a map.

The map fascinated me, as if by just looking at it I might discover who held the command. I studied it too, trying to perceive why the place was so vital. Still, I could learn nothing more, save that the fort was far away and situated where the river was narrow. I concluded that the narrowness of the river meant West Point could command all river passage north and south. No wonder it was so vital.

I also searched out the location of Oyster Bay, thinking I might go *there* in search of Mr. Townsend. I found it some thirty miles out upon the northern coast of Long Island. Yes, closer than West Point. But if something had happened to Mr. Townsend, he might not be there. I kept telling myself—desperately wanting, I should say—that I would see Mr. Townsend soon. Else, what was I to do with what I knew?

At the same time, I began to ponder how to act if he failed to come. What if, as might be truly the case, he'd been arrested? Perhaps he was being held on a prison ship in Wallabout Bay. Or even hung?

All too ghastly to believe.

I told myself I must be patient, but in truth, my anxiety was constantly mounting. What if, in this waiting time, "Mr. Moore" found a way to give West Point to the British? The war would be lost.

Like Indian corn in August, the "what ifs" in my life were growing fast. Too fast.

❖ **48** ❖

THEN, DURING THE third week of July, I found another letter from "Mr. Moore" on André's desk. In sum, "Mr. Moore" insisted upon a meeting with Mr. Anderson. I now had two mysteries: Who was Mr. Moore? Who was Mr. Anderson?

A few days later, I found a new memorandum on André's desk. Written in *his* hand, it was marked, "For Moore. To be coded by Odell." There! That was Odell's role—a coder. In part, André had written:

> *Tho West Point derives its importance from the nature*
> *of the operations of our enemy yet should we thro*
> *your means possesses ourselves of 3,000 men and its*
> *artillery and stores with the magazine of provisions*
> *for the army which may probably be there the sum of*
> *20,000 pounds should be paid you.*

It was signed, "Anderson."

Anderson is André! A huge discovery! Moreover, André was offering a vast sum of money—a sum far greater than I had seen mentioned before—if the British gained possession of West Point from "Mr. Moore."

Thus it was, the most critical question of all still remained: Who was "Mr. Moore"?

I felt the information I already had—unless revealed to someone—would explode inside of me. Even so, I still heard nothing from Mr. Townsend. Ever more desperate, I left another message for "Culper" at the Kings Crown to the effect that I *must* see him.

No response came.

During one night in the second half of August, I came home tired from work and extremely dejected with the inactivity in this desperate matter. As it happened, Father was still up, reading. We exchanged a few words, but he must have sensed my mood, for he took pains to cheer me.

"Your mother's friend," he said, "Mistress Lorenz, was here this afternoon. She brought her whole budget of gossip. Some of it was news that should cheer you."

"What was it?"

"You were asking about that place, West Point. Remember, I was telling you how important it was."

I looked up. "What news could she have?"

"West Point will be safe."

"Why? What do you mean?"

"You'll be pleased to know that—according to her—your hero has taken command of it."

"My hero? What hero is that?"

"General Arnold."

Astonished, I managed to say, "Are you sure she said

his name? That it's Arnold who . . . is in charge of West Point?"

He smiled. "Your mother will confirm it."

"But is it fact?"

He laughed. "That woman seems to know things. I trust her more than those Tory newspapers for which I work."

What I felt was nothing less than utter confusion.

Arnold in command of West Point.

I *should* have felt that West Point was now safe, because Benedict Arnold, our very best general, the patriot hero of Montreal, Fort Ticonderoga, Lake Champlain, and Saratoga was in command. *My* hero!

I should have been overjoyed that it was *not* "Mr. Moore" who was in command.

Nevertheless, I had told myself that to uncover who "Mr. Moore" actually was, I needed only to discover who was in command of West Point.

By all logic, "Mr. Moore" was America's most successful general, Benedict Arnold. And he was selling West Point to the British.

49

I SAT THERE, refusing to believe what I had just heard: Arnold was Mr. Moore. Inconceivable! Monstrous! Confounding! Too terrifying as to its import.

Besides, if it was the truth—which I *had* to doubt—what could I do with such appalling intelligence? That Mr. Townsend had vanished at such a time only added to my dread.

Then I thought, even if I could tell him my news, I was not sure he would believe me. Why should he when I myself could hardly give it the color of truth!

I fairly moaned with exasperation.

I recalled Mr. Townsend telling me he provided information for General Washington. I imagined myself seeking out the general and telling him directly what I had learned. That too was absurd. I did not know where he was. Had no idea how to reach him. Besides, would he actually listen to a girl?

Then I remembered Mr. Townsend saying he gave *his* information to a Connecticut man, someone named Tallmadge. Alas, I knew no more know about this Tallmadge than the man in the moon.

In short, there was nothing for me to do but keep my horrific discoveries within me and wait upon Mr. Townsend. When he did come—I kept telling myself—he probably would assure me my worries were for naught.

People know of the danger of spying. Yes, it is hard to discover a truth. But it is much harder to be unable to do anything about it. It's as if you know for certain a building will collapse and not one soul—not even those within—will listen to your warning. Hearing truth makes many deaf.

During this same period, some noteworthy things did happen. The first was that the Kennedy house became abuzz with the news that John André had been promoted to Major General. There was much speculation among the cleaning maids and kitchen staff as to why this had happened. Some said it was because he was a special favorite of General Clinton. Others insisted it was because he had distinguished himself at the Siege of Charleston. Some claimed he had wheedled the rise with his famous charm. Then there was the suggestion that most interested me: that the new Major General was engaged upon a secret endeavor to end the war swiftly. As to what that enterprise exactly was, no one knew.

Alas, I was certain *I* did know, knew it too well.

Just to think that John André was in the center of this almost drove me to distraction. Why must it be him?

The other event of weight that occurred was the

Battle of Camden, in South Carolina. It proved a disaster for the Americans under General Gates. The Americans' biggest defeat yet, or so it was bragged at British headquarters. The talk became ever more insistent that the war must, with certainty, be over soon. Would William and countless others have died for nothing?

Typically, one of my work companions gossiped, "One more stroke and it shall be done." She even added, "And I'm sure it'll be Major André who brings it off."

How ghastly to hear that. And yet, I confess it—that horror was touched with high regard. Why should it not be him?

Then on the last day of August, I came upon a new letter on André's desk. Addressed to "Mr. John Anderson, Merchant," it was written in a hand I did not recognize. One part that caught my absolute attention:

> *... in a few days ... to procure you an interview with Mr. Moore when you will be able to settle your commercial plan I hope agreeable to all parties, Mr. Moore assures me that he is still of opinion that his first proposal is by no means unreasonable and makes no doubt when he has a conference with you that you will close with it. He expects when you meet that you will be fully authorized from your house: that the risks and profit of the co-partnership may be full and clearly understood.*

It closed by saying:

> Mr. Moore flatters himself that in the course
> of ten days he will have the pleasure of
> seeing you.

To the best of my abilities, based on everything I had learned, Arnold ("Moore") was to meet André ("Anderson") and deliver West Point to him. This meeting was crucial for the betrayal, for at this meeting, Arnold wished to negotiate the price of his treason.

In *ten* days!

I was absolutely distracted. I must *do* something but knew not how to even begin. The best I could do was watch André, observe what he did closely, which I did. And pray Mr. Townsend would appear.

It was then—no coincidence, I was convinced—that a squadron of ten British war ships arrived and anchored in the lower bay. Troops went on board. House gossip claimed they were heading south. I believed they were going the other way, northward, to West Point.

Oh, where was Mr. Townsend! Why would he vanish at such a time? I was so angry with him. I began to think my only choice was to walk to Oyster Bay.

Then, to my complete frustration, Mrs. Ticknor informed me that since Sir Henry Clinton was going to Beekman Mansion to escape the heat, I, along with other house staff, must go with him. Upon the instant, what went through my head was the memory that

Beekman Mansion was where General Howe had condemned Nathan Hale to death.

There was much more: in a stroke, my ability to watch John André was erased just when the treacherous meeting with Arnold was to take place. In a matter of days.

Did my despair matter? Not a jot. On the night before we departed for Beekman Mansion I went home along Broadway, wishing only that Mr. Townsend would appear. He did not.

Though I knew for a certainty that a frightful event was about to take place, I had been rendered utterly useless.

Do you wonder that as I lay down to sleep I wept? All, all was for naught.

⟡ 50 ⟡

BEEKMAN MANSION WAS a large, graceful building a few miles north of the city. When the British occupied New York it was taken first by General Howe and then by General Clinton. I knew hardly anything of its past, save that it was where Nathan Hale had his so-called trial.

Though General Clinton and his officers went along on horseback, we six female servants went by jolting wagon. I was certain I had lost all contact with André and Arnold's plot. Indeed, I have must have appeared so forlorn, one of my companions asked me if had been jilted by a suitor.

In a sense, I had.

Once at the mansion, I was told that another girl and I would serve table. During that first night, when I brought in the soup, I found that seated at the table was Major John André.

Can you imagine my astonishment?

Dressed as smartly as ever, he wore a red jacket with gold facings and green trim. His wig was powdered snow white. If he recognized me from the Kennedy house, he gave no sign. Of course, he would hardly have bothered to notice the likes of me. I cannot say which I felt most—resentment or joy.

That first dinner was a relaxed affair, with talk of refined matters: a play performed in the city's Theatre Royal, the latest gossip from London, an officers' ball planned in the city. Major André even recited a poem he had written that mocked American soldiers, a poem being published in Mr. Gaine's *Mercury*. It was the only mention of the war and it brought much laughter.

Once the formal dinner was over and the women withdrew from the table, General Clinton, Major André, and a certain Colonel Beverly Robinson remained.

I had seen Colonel Robinson at headquarters. American born, he had joined the British ranks months ago. He did more, leading a regiment called the Loyal Americans—loyal, that is, to King George.

The talk among these men shifted to military matters. In fact, when I brought in the silver coffeepot, I heard them speaking about the coming meeting between Major André and General Arnold. Among the three, Arnold's name was bandied about openly. Though shocking, I found it satisfying that *I* had previously discovered most of it on my own.

What were they saying?

A meeting of Arnold and André was to happen at a place called Dobbs Ferry, a community up Hudson's River. Recalling the maps I had studied at the Kennedy house, I knew this was in the general direction of West Point.

André mentioned that Arnold wished him *not* to wear his uniform at the meeting, but come disguised as a merchant named John Anderson. Anderson, of course, was the name André used to communicate with Arnold.

"I don't care what name you use," General Clinton scolded, "but under no circumstance, Major, shall you remove your uniform. The danger is too great."

"You know how it is," Robinson agreed. "Be captured in your uniform, and you will be treated as an officer. Without a uniform, you'll be considered a spy."

A smiling André promised to follow the order. Then, quite casually, he announced that General Arnold had suggested that there was a good chance that when they took West Point they would be able to capture General Washington.

Though André spoke offhandedly, there was a potent pause after this remark. *General Washington captured!* Even I stopped my serving.

"If we do that," said Clinton, "it will absolutely end the war."

"God grant it," said Colonel Robinson.

"For all of this to work," General Clinton instructed André, "surprise is crucial. Once you confer with Arnold, you *must* retreat to the city as fast as possible. Troops are already waiting to begin the attack upon the fort."

How hard for me to keep my self-control and still serve.

Though I dawdled, I learned no more. When I brought more coffee to the room, they had moved on to other matters.

That night, in the stifling attic of the house, in the narrow bed I shared with another girl, I all but boiled with frustration. I was much like the person who labors forever at planning a voyage, draws detailed maps, packs trunks—yet goes nowhere. I was failing my brother and my country. Of course, I slept but poorly.

In the morning, I learned that André and Robinson had gone off, presumably to that Dobbs Ferry.

But among the many desperate emotions that churned within me, the strongest was *rage*, rage at myself. Never mind what I had discovered. What had I done? *Nothing*.

It would have been easy to excuse myself by claiming the cause of my inaction was Mr. Townsend's absence, which was none of my doing. Yet there I was, aware that General Arnold was about to commit horrible treason— treason that, in all likelihood, would lose the war for my country. What did I do? Serve food and wash dishes!

In such a state, I made a vow. I told myself that *if*, by some miracle, the meeting *was* in some way or fashion foiled, I must, given a second chance, do *something*.

Dear Reader:

From this point forward in my history, I will recount some events I did not see for myself, but learned about later from what people told me, plus the many things written and said after the actions.

With this understood, let me relate how things stood.

Sophia Calderwood

✦ 51 ✦

GENERAL ARNOLD AND Major André were trying to meet at Dobbs Ferry. The town was situated upon Hudson's River, above Manhattan, some thirty-five miles below West Point in an area known as the neutral territory. It was called "neutral" since neither British or American forces controlled it. To the north were Americans. To the south, British. Thus, in popular jabber, Americans were styled "the upper party," whereas the British were called "the lower party."

The words and distinctions would have considerable import.

As planned, on September eleventh, André went up to Dobbs Ferry. Under a white flag of truce, he waited for Arnold. I could have no doubt: during this meeting, Arnold intended to provide André with the means of giving Fort West Point to the British.

You can guess then, my shock, as well as my elation, when the next day, September twelfth, John André was restored to Beekman Mansion and General Clinton. Only when I served them did I learn that the meeting with Arnold had *not* taken place.

What had happened? It appeared that Arnold—as planned—had a party of men row him down the river. As I have told you, the meeting was a secret. Indeed, it was so secret that a British gunboat, a few of which patrolled the river north of New York to watch American military movement, fired on Arnold, driving his boat back to shore—the shore opposite where André was waiting.

Thus, it fell out that the British themselves prevented the fateful meeting!

André was extremely frustrated. Nonetheless, he, Clinton, and Robinson discussed finding another way to meet Arnold.

Though I did not see the letters, André and Arnold must have managed to communicate. Arrangements for a *new* meeting were made. This plan was that André would board the *Vulture*, a British armed sloop that patrolled Hudson's River, and sail up to a place called Tellers Point. How fitting, I thought, for the boat to be named after such a grasping bird!

Once the *Vulture* arrived on September fifteenth, Arnold would send a small boat for André. At that meeting, Arnold would tell André how best to conquer West Point. André would then reboard the *Vulture* and sail to New York City. With strategy in hand, the attack on West Point would commence.

Such was their plan.

Once again, I heard General Clinton tell André: when he met Arnold, he *must* stay in uniform. He further cautioned André not to go beyond the neutral territory, into

American lines, or carry any incriminating documents.

André, with his charming smile, promised he would do as told.

When I heard them making this new plan, I recalled the vow *I* had made. Having been provided with a *second* chance to prevent the meeting of André and Arnold, I felt obliged to act. But how was I, a maid of fifteen, to array herself against such powerful men? It was not as if I had a plan, some powers, or even allies to go against these conspirators. There I was, far above the city. I knew not one person with whom I might confide.

On Friday the fifteenth, Major André and Colonel Robinson took a small sailboat up to the *Vulture*, which lay upon Hudson's River.

The knowledge that they had done so made me deplore my helplessness. I loathed myself.

You may picture my bepuzzlement when, next day, I learned that this second meeting had not taken place either! Once again, some communication between Arnold and André must have occurred. For, having failed to reach the *Vulture*—I never knew why—Arnold promised that next time he would send a man named Joshua Smith to the *Vulture*, which would be anchored off that place called Tellers Point.

This Mr. Smith was the brother of the loyalist chief justice in New York City. Despite—or perhaps because of—this connection, Smith was a self-proclaimed patriot. Which is to say he was vague in his allegiance, and moved between both camps with ease. I don't pretend to know his motives, I only know it was so.

It was Mr. Smith who would bring André ashore to Arnold. This *third* attempt at meeting would occur on the twentieth of September. Three days hence.

At this point, though you may consider it vast vanity, *I* came to believe that what had occurred was evidence of the hand of Providence.

Twice I had resolved to do something to block the treason.

Twice I failed to act, unable to think of what I might do. Yet the treason had not yet taken place.

Do you wonder that I should believe that Providence was *demanding* I take action? This time, I committed myself—*absolutely*—to do something. It all came down to this: I was the *only* patriot in America who knew the extreme danger our country was facing. How could I *not* act? Moreover, I had but three days to do so.

❖ 52 ❖

I HAD NOT thought out a plan. Far from it. I only knew if I were to save West Point, I must somehow prevent André and Arnold from meeting. Failing that, I must go to West Point itself and tell someone what was happening. In short, other than first getting to Tellers Point, I had no strategy.

Therefore, it was on the night of September sixteenth, a Saturday, when my housework was done and my companions had gone to sleep in that hot and airless attic, that I rose from my bed. I dressed myself, crept down the servants' steps, and left Beekman Mansion by way of a back door.

To reach West Point, I needed to go fifty miles. In my favor was this: I had spent much time in Major André's office looking at maps. That study had given me a general sense of the land that lay between Manhattan and West Point, the area known as the Hudson Valley.

I knew, of course, that Manhattan was an island. I knew I must, at some point, cross water. I was aware of the fact that the narrowest crossing was at Manhattan's northern end. Furthermore, West Point was on the western side of Hudson's River. In other words, I had *two* bodies of water to get over. I did not know how to swim.

Was ever so vital a journey taken with so many hugger-mugger thoughts! In truth, it was midsummer madness garbed in bits of bravery. But then, as someone said, All beginnings have wings of vanity. If that was so, I had taken flight with enormous wings.

I do not know what time I left the mansion, save that a bright half-moon provided enough light to guide me over rolling hills. Warm air, blessed with a slight breeze, kept me fresh. A few paths helped. Twice I passed roads, but they ran north-south and I was heading west. Occasionally, a grasshopper leaped, wings clacking to keep me alert. Glowflies resparkled here and there. Crickets chirruped. I heard foretelling owls, but what their hoots predicted I knew not.

The first dab of dawn had arrived when I reached Hudson's River. The river was so much wider than the East River. In the early light I could not see across, but I could smell the river's ripe expanse. Hudson's River being tidal, the ocean reaches far inland with strong tides and the pungent smells of sea.

It was upon sensing the river's vastness that I fully grasped the enormous compass—not to say goosery— of my enterprise. That said, my determination was so locked I could hardly pry it apart. Did I not have energy, strength, and most of all, motive? Reminding myself I had but three days, I began to walk northward.

As morning light grew, I observed the far Jersey shore, with its steep cliffs, an impassable barrier. I was traveling on the eastern shore, where the river quietly lapped a low beach. That beach was mostly pebbly, though now and again there were boulders, which I had to climb or circumvent. Here and there lay tangles of gray driftwood, while multitudes of white oyster shells paved the way. I heard no sounds save my munching steps, occasional squawking gulls, and shrieking terns. Once I caught sight of a big fish leaping and splashing down.

After about an hour's walk, I had what I thought was a stroke of luck: I smelled burning wood. Mingled with that smell was the distinct scent of cooking fish. Coming round a bend, I espied a small fire burning near the water's edge. Hauled upon the beach was what I took to be an old whaleboat, no more than twenty feet long, its single sail lowered. Nearby were a man and a woman, an elderly couple.

Tending the fire, cooking in an iron pot by stirring with a wooden spoon, the woman wore a sullied apron over an ankle-length and much-patched dress. A floppy cap sat over long, gray, and tangled hair. She wore no shoes.

Close by, the man sat cross-legged, mending a fishing net. He was bald, with a fringe of gray hair and spiky white whiskers. A buff jacket was on his back, a frayed cloth round his neck, and old, lumpy boots on his feet.

Not sure if I had anything to fear from such people, I approached with caution.

"Good morning to you, mistress," I called from a distance.

The woman squinted at me. "Good morning to you."
The man offered a curt nod.

Without ceasing her stirring, the woman said, "Do you live nearby?"

"In the city."

"Miles 'way from home, then."

I said, "And further to go."

"Where's that?"

The first thing that popped out of my mouth was "Tellers Point."

"A fair ways," said the man.

I stood there looking at them, uncertain how to proceed, wondering what I should say if they asked more questions.

"What's at the point?" the woman asked.

"My mother is ill," I said, surprised how easily the lie—without thought—came to my lips.

The woman stirred her pot awhile and then said, "Best come and eat, then."

I sat upon the ground and was handed a wooden bowl of fish, which was pleasing. As we ate, the woman told me that they had been to the city to sell dried salmon, that her name was Bente, her husband's name Johan, their family name Vanzandt—Dutch.

I warned myself to speak with care, since Dutch New Yorkers were said to be loyalists.

At length Bente asked, "What ails your mother?"

"They just said she was ill," I said.

Johan said. "Do you mean to walk the whole way?"

"I must."

"We're fisherfolk," said Bente. "From upriver. Rhine-beck town."

"Going home," added Johan. "Just waiting till the tide shifts. The river rises four, five feet with the tide," he explained. "Hard to go against it."

I said nothing.

Then Johan added, "It'll take you three days to walk to Tellers Point. What'll you do for food?"

Embarrassed not to have even thought of such a thing, I stayed mum.

Bente reached out, tapped my knee with a crooked finger, and said, "You'd best come with us. What's your name?"

"Molly Saville," I said, offering the old lie with ease.

Thus it was settled that I'd sail up river with them.

Even as I agreed to travel with them, John André was arranging yet again to sail up the same river to that British sloop the *Vulture*, from which Mr. Smith would fetch him.

53

THOUGH I WAS eager to depart, it was necessary to wait till the river tide flooded north. Moreover, despite being very tired, I dared not sleep, worried they would leave without me. As it happened, it took some hours before Johan announced, "We can go."

After loading their few possessions—kettle and fishing equipment—we pushed the boat into the water. Bente and I scrambled in while Johan shoved until he was up to his waist, then clambered aboard.

While I sat down in the bottom, amidships, Bente hoisted a triangular sail—a lateen rig—up the short mast. Johan took the stern, hand upon the tiller, which he shifted. The boat turned and the gray and patched canvas stiffened with breeze. We heeled slightly, righted ourselves, and began to move in a northerly direction.

Johan maneuvered the small boat until she ran a middle course upriver. Not that we went fast or in a straight line. The wind, hedged in by the cliffs on the western bank of the river, as well as the forest on the eastern, was erratic. Johan tacked constantly, but the zigzags brought us upriver.

Happily, the couple did not talk much. Rather, Johan concentrated on his steering, while Bente threw out a fishing line and put her attention to that. I spent my time gazing upon the shore.

It was a hot and humid day with a haze hugging the river, softening the light. Here and there, horse-stingers darted cross the water's surface. Once, at the river's edge, I saw a buck with many-pronged antlers that had come down to drink among the drooping tree leaves, leaves already tinged with autumn reds.

Convinced I would now reach West Point in time, I allowed myself to relax. As we sailed north, the steady *slip-slap* of the bow teased me to sleep. Only when Johan abruptly called out, "Ship ahead!" did I awaken.

Sitting up, I looked where he pointed.

Upriver I saw a one-masted ship with a square topsail and large mizzen sail furled on her single mast and boom. Facing north, she lay quietly in the water, riding so calmly I presumed she was at anchor. Along her port quarterdeck, I counted six small cannon muzzles. From her stern hung a limp flag, so enfolded I could not determine who it was. A few people were on her deck.

"What is she?" I asked.

"The *Vulture*," said Johan. "British. She patrols the river here about. Captain Sutherland commands."

Openmouthed, I realized that this was the same ship that John André was intending to board to meet Arnold.

Thinking that perhaps André might already be on board, I tried to imagine what *he* might do if he knew *I* was on this tiny boat trying to keep him from his appointment. André and I, hiding from each other, equally deceitful but bent upon opposite goals.

Fearful, I turned to Johan. "Will she stop us?" I asked. "Board us?"

I suspect my face betrayed anxiety, for the old man gazed at me with more intensity than he'd shown before. "You needn't be concerned," he said. "Captain Sutherland knows me."

I wished I had not spoken.

As we drew even with the *Vulture*, Johan lifted an arm in greeting. Someone on the deck answered the salute. For my part, I turned away and could not help trying to make myself small.

As we sailed northward, Johan stole glances at me, as if trying to discover something. Though fearful I'd given myself away, there was nothing I could do.

We sailed on. At some places, the river broadened greatly. Other places it narrowed. On both shores, the land rose high. When I gazed upriver, I began to see highlands, a few peaks crowned in gloomy clouds. As the day wore on, these clouds began to spread and fill the sky. Then the wind freshened and bore a ripe, earthy smell, the scent of rain. Ripples fluttered the river's surface.

"Squall coming," Johan announced, and aimed his boat toward the eastern shore.

Fretful, my unspoken thought was *I'm losing time*.

As we ground against a stony beach, rain began to patter. We hauled the boat high, left it, and then threaded ourselves among the dense trees until we found a spot protected by a canopy of branches. By then the rain was pelting.

Bente and I scurried about in search of fallen wood. It was she, using flint, spark, and breath, who expertly lit a fire. During that time I had slept on the boat, she must have caught a salmon. Now she cleaned it with a knife and proceeded to cook it.

The rain came harder. A sudden crack of lightning made me jump. Moments later, lumbering thunder came, followed by even heaver rain. Water dripped in silver sheets.

For some hours, we waited beneath that storm. In time, it moved on, leaving the air as sweet as Adam's first day. By then, however, it was night, and the tide had turned.

"No farther today," Johan announced.

We sat before the smoky, sparky fire. My damp clothing itched. No one spoke. At one point, however, Johan abruptly said, "Tell me, girl, what's in the city that you're running from?"

"Nothing, sir," I answered truthfully, relieved when he asked no more. But sensing that he *had* become suspicious, I wished my time with them were done. Should I slip into the forest? Alas, though I had little knowledge as to where we were, or how far from West Point, I realized I had but two days left to stop Arnold from meeting André. I therefore resolved to stay with these people as long as I might manage it.

❖ 54 ❖

HAVING SLEPT ON damp ground, we awoke at dawn,
the nineteenth of September. For breakfast we ate
what remained of the fish from the night before.
There was not much talk as we waited for Johan to
announce that the tide was flooding in our favor.
Meanwhile, I kept out of his way by bailing water
from the boat.

When Johan pronounced us ready, we pushed the
boat back into the river, climbed in, raised the sail, and
kept heading north. I was much relieved.

In New York City, His Excellency General Henry Clinton
sent orders to his troops on the transport ships to be
ready to make an assault in a few days' time. He told
Admiral Rodney that the attack would be upon Fort
West Point but asked that he keep it a secret.

General Arnold was having difficulties finding the
means to reach the *Vulture*. Unable to secure a boat or
find rowers, the meeting with André had to be put off
yet another night.

The Vanzandts and I sailed for about an hour beneath a bright morning sky. It was already warm.

I said, "How far have we come?"

Johan answered, "'Bout twenty miles south of your Tellers Point."

That pleased me.

Johan was quiet for an interval, but then said, "You seem a good girl, miss. All the same, I sense something wrong. You need tell me what it is."

Bente shifted around expectantly.

Taken by surprise, I said, "It's what I said. My mother is ill."

"So you say. But yesterday, when we passed the *Vulture*, you were frightened. Why's that? Made me think you were running away from something."

"No, sir," I insisted. "I'm not."

It was a while before he suddenly said, "Where are you in this awful war?"

Fearful that no good would come of any answer I might make, I stayed silent and would not even look at him.

He said, "I don't ask it of you—you're a girl—but your father. I suppose you have one. You said you came from the city. What did you do there?"

"A housemaid, sir."

He seemed to accept my answer, but then said, "I want nothing to do with this rebellion. I stand with the king. We had some land and cattle. The rebels stole it all when I wouldn't pledge to their new government."

I said, "I'm sorry to hear it, sir."

He remained silent for a while, so that I thought his mood had passed. Instead, he leaned toward me and said, "Which side do you wish to be?"

"Side?" I said, thinking he meant which side of *politics*.

"Which side of the river," he said. "I won't carry rebel folk. If you'll not declare with me, you must be against." He gave a brusque nod as if agreeing with himself.

Not waiting for my reply, he abruptly shifted the tiller, causing the boat to sail toward the nearest shore, which was to the east.

I didn't know what to say.

In moments we jolted against the shore. "Out, then," he commanded.

I gazed about. Beyond the slim shingle of stone and rock lay thick forest. I appealed to Bente with a glance, but she would not lift her eyes to mine.

Johan said, "It's not so far that you can't walk the rest. Out!"

I stepped into the shallow, warm water and went on the land. Johan leaped from the boat too, but only to push it back out. He hauled himself in, turned the tiller, and without so much as a glance, sailed his boat away. Only then did Bente turn toward me, her face offering distress. Dismayed, I watched as the couple moved upriver until they passed from my view.

As I stood there on the shore, my breath coming with difficulty, I tried to recover my dizzy wits, quiet my heart, and sort out my circumstance. With but poor knowledge of where I was or what I might do, I felt marooned. Had I had been folly-blind to undertake this venture?

After some time had passed, I became calmer. I reminded myself that I had already come a long way. Moreover, there were less than *two* days until André's meeting. Did not Johan say I was close to Tellers Point, that I might walk the rest? True, I was not sure how many miles Tellers Point was from West Point but had hopes I could reach it.

Having composed myself, I considered where I was. Before me ran the wide river. The opposite shore was nothing but forest, which rose like a wall. Behind me, the trees were equally thick, making the interior impossible to observe at any depth. Moreover, I had been left in a small cove, so I could not see north or south.

Yet I knew I could not remain where I was. That said, I was fearful of the forest and what might lurk within: savage animals, or people who might do me harm.

In short, the river was the sole road I knew. Little choice then but to continue moving north along its edge.

I set off.

❖ 55 ❖

THERE IS THAT expression "as the arrow flies," which, presumably, means "straight." You might contrast that with the phrase "as Sophia walked." For I went every which way but straight. The undulations of the river shoreline were as jagged as handsaw teeth. I made progress northward, but never directly.

More often than not, I simply tried to follow the water's edge, in and out, though now and again I attempted to wade across the many inlets, shoes in hand. In many places, the water was shallow, no higher than my knees. But sometimes the bottom dropped off sharply, forcing a retreat, so I must creep round that spot. Once, twice, I slipped, fell, and became soaked. I shook myself like a wet dog and went on. With my dress—dirty, damp, and torn in a few places—I must have appeared (if anyone were there to see) like a female Robinson Crusoe.

Three times I saw paths that led from the water's edge into the forest. Once I came upon what I supposed was a landing. A broken boat lay to one side. Of people or houses I saw none, though I startled a raccoon that had come to the river's edge to wash its food. How I wished I had food to wash! I saw no oysters but was sometimes cheered by flowers, goldenrod and purple asters, and countless flaming maple trees.

How many hours I edged northward in such a fashion, I cannot say, but in time daylight dimmed to dusk. I searched and found a sandy patch between large boulders. Miserably cramped, damp, hungry, and weary, I tried to settle down.

As I lay there, night crickets creaked unceasingly and the river water jabbled. I gazed upon the stars in the vast black sky, and the half-moon, which gilded the river's surface with a rippling golden hue. *Will I be in time?* I kept asking myself. I could not help wondering where John André was at that moment. Thinking of him, ever gallant, splendid in his uniform, handsome, self-assured, and eager to attack, to destroy my country, I fell asleep.

At Beekman Mansion, a restless Major André kept talking to Colonel Robinson, speculating why General Arnold had failed their two previous appointments.

"Then you think he'll really come?" said Robinson.

"He's committed himself," said André.

He and Robinson mused about what would be achieved when the assault of West Point took place. "I intend to ask General Clinton to let me lead the attack," said André.

"He's bound to let you. Of course, it will be successful. Arnold must make it happen."

André said, "The capture of the fort will bring an end to the war."

"And," added Robinson with a grin, "glory, promotion, and wealth for you. I suppose the king will bestow a title. And you only twenty-nine years old."

André paced the mansion, waiting for the next morning, when a small sailboat would take him up the river to the *Vulture*, and to Arnold.

⋄ 56 ⋄

ON WEDNESDAY MORNING, September twentieth, I
awoke cold, bone sore, and very hungry. Forest, river,
rocks, plus a wilderness of ignorance, surrounded me.
For a while, I remained where I was, in painful melancholy. But I knew the reality. Not to continue would be
fatal in all respects.

I roused myself and walked as the day before, along
the river's edge. I went in, out, across modest inlets and
small creeks, but always, always, I moved north.

In Beekman Mansion, Major John André, assisted by
Peter Laune, his servant, dressed with care. It was
imperative to André that when he met General Arnold
he appear at his best. He would be representing the
British Army. Everything he did, the way he appeared
and talked, the way he dealt with others, would help to
establish his authority, dignity, and power. It was not
just an honor to wear the uniform; he would be representing the greatest nation on earth.

Besides, as André was well aware, General Arnold,
despite his reputation as a good military man, was

not a gentleman, merely a colonial merchant. When André came face-to-face with him, he must assert his superiority from the first. There was something amusing too about the fact that Arnold had married Peggy Shippen, the girl André had flirted with when he was in Philadelphia.

As André stood before his looking glass, musing, adjusting his wig, there was a knock on his dressing room door. André's servant opened it. A soldier stood in the hallway. "Sir," he said, saluting, while addressing Major André, "the boat you requested to take you and Colonel Robinson to the *Vulture* is ready."

"Thank you."

André's servant shut the door. "Sir, may I take the liberty of asking where you are going?"

"Just a pleasant excursion, Peter," said André. "I'll be back very soon."

I don't know how far I walked. Save for a handful of blackberries, I ate nothing. They colored my hands red, as if I were a murderess caught in the act. The dye reminded me of the black ink from Mr. Gaine's printing press. Those days seemed far beyond.

As I made my way, I began to perceive that directly north was a large extension of land that reached far into the river. Having no idea what it meant for my journey, I simply pressed on. As the day wore, however, I began to grasp that the land I'd seen had a shoreline that cut in deeply in an easterly direction.

I soon came upon the mouth of a wide inlet, far too

wide for me to wade across. Looking eastward, up the inlet, I saw I would have to go a goodly distance eastward before I could even consider crossing over.

The thought of such a detour wearied me. Would I never get there? In truth, I no longer really knew where *there* was!

At 7 p.m., Major André and Colonel Robinson reached the *Vulture*. Captain Sutherland welcomed them aboard again and showed them to a small cabin where a simple dinner awaited. Leaving his guests to their food, the captain ordered the ship's sails be hoisted, the anchor lifted. Slowly, the *Vulture* began to move upriver toward its appointed meeting place off Tellers Point.

In expectation of André's arrival, General Arnold went to the home of Mr. Joshua Hett Smith. It sat twenty miles south of West Point, on the western bank of Hudson's River. Situated on a bluff, it had a good view of Tellers Point. Moreover, it was not far from the shore point— Long Clove Mountain cove—where Arnold planned to meet André.

Arnold ordered Smith to find a boat and rowers, telling his friend that he was meeting a valued business visitor, a Mr. Anderson. Mr. Smith, having learned that safety for him in the war meant asking no questions, agreed to go to the *Vulture.* It would be anchored off Tellers Point. Mr. Anderson was on board. At midnight, Smith would convey the gentleman to shore. Arnold would meet him. Such was the plan.

Arnold was satisfied that this time the meeting would absolutely take place.

Tired, hungry, and dejected, having no idea where I was, I sat down upon a boulder and gazed upon Hudson's River. It was quite wide at that spot. The evening was hot. Mosquito flies buzzed my ears. I told myself I should take a short nap and then push on. I lay down, closed my eyes, and slept.

As I slept, the *Vulture* sailed right by me. When it reached Tellers Point, its anchor splashed down and held. Waiting for Arnold or his messenger to arrive, André walked the deck with Colonel Robinson.

Onshore, Mr. Smith was having a difficult time recruiting rowers to take him to the ship. It was unfortunate, but General Arnold and Mr. Anderson would have to wait until the next night to meet.

❖ 57 ❖

I AWOKE WITH a jolt only to realize I had slept through the night. Springing to my feet, I looked around. To the north was a ship. It took but a moment for me to recognize the *Vulture*.

I stared at it with consternation. Had the meeting of Arnold and André already taken place? Might André still be on the ship? Frantic, I hastened eastward along the shore of that wide inlet, walking, running, sometimes, in my haste, stumbling.

After a while, I began to grasp that I was not moving along an inlet but the mouth of yet another river. A wide river. While I could see that in the far distance it was narrowing, I was unsure at what point I would be able to cross.

I had gone, perhaps, half an hour, constantly balked, and hot beneath the sun, when I spied two men by the river's bank. I halted.

They were sitting side by side on the trunk of an old tree. Close was a canoe. What's more, these men were in uniform. Soldiers. Yes, I could see that they were not *red* uniforms but blue ones. Even so, I didn't know what to do. With my exhaustion and frustration, I was hardly capable of determining uniforms. I believed—or wanted to believe—that they were from the American army, but I dared not trust my judgment. If wrong, all would be lost. In my befuddlement, I even wondered, recalling that the *Vulture* was not so far away, that perhaps one of these men was General Arnold.

As a result, I simply stood where I was, gawking. Before I could make up my mind what to do, one of the soldiers spied me and jumped up. His companion did the same. That one held a musket. Both wore blue jackets with bands of white across their chests. They stood there staring at me. But then, they could have no idea where I came from. With my dress disordered, soiled, and torn, my face and hair the same, I might as well have been a witch.

My first thought was that I should run away. However, you must believe me when I say it was not courage but utter fatigue that made me call out, "Who are you?"

The soldier who had first stood answered, "Philip Groogins." He was a young man.

"Richard Baydon," said the other, middle-aged.

Poised to flee, I said, "What army do you belong to?"

"The upper party," said the young one. "American."

"From Fort Lafayette," said the one name Baydon. He nodded cross the river.

"Under the command of Colonel James Livingston," Mr. Baydon went on when I said nothing. "Who are you?"

"Miss Molly Saville. I must speak with your commander."

"Why?" They seemed truly bewildered.

Though unsure what to say, I could not hold myself back. "Something awful is about to happen," I cried out.

"What?"

The direct question unnerved me. Who was I to trust? I said, "I can only inform your officer."

They studied me. It was Mr. Groogins who said, "You need to tell us *something*."

I pointed back from where I had come. "There's a British ship out there. The *Vulture*. Just north of the land. Off some point."

"Tellers Point?"

"I suppose," I said, only then realizing I had come close to where I wished to be. "She's bringing a spy."

They exchanged looks before turning back to me.

"Where do you come from?" asked Mr. Baydon.

"New York City."

Again they just gazed as if not believing me. Mr. Groogins said, "From British lines?"

"Please," I said. "It's urgent. Your commander needs to know about that ship and the spy. You must take me to him."

"It's some miles north."

"I don't care!" I cried, increasingly exasperated.

"You sure about what you said?"

"I beg you! You can see the ship for yourself. Please, it's urgent!"

The two conferred in private voices, now and again

glancing in my direction as if uncertain what to make of me. I suspect they thought me daft, and must do *something* on that account, if for no other reason.

"All right," said Mr. Baydon. "We'll take you. Come along."

They went to their canoe, picked it up, and set in the river, then beckoned me to join them. I got in while they pushed it out.

With strong paddle strokes, we crossed the river. As we went, I said, "Where are we?"

"This is the Croton River. Over there—" Mr. Baydon paused. "Do you really not know where you are?"

"Only a bit."

"Then how did you get here?"

"Some fisherfolk took me part of the way from Manhattan Island in their boat. For the rest I walked."

"*Alone?*" said Mr. Groogins.

I nodded.

The two exchanged looks of doubt but said no more.

Once we had crossed the river, they set their canoe among trees where I supposed it would not be readily seen.

Mr. Baydon said, "This way." With him in the lead, and the younger soldier behind me—I think they were guarding me—we started walking along a wide path that went through the forest.

✦ 58 ✦

IT WAS A long march, but not difficult, the path being fairly even and the trees by which we walked thick enough that it shielded us from the sun. We barely talked. I did ask them where they came from. "Jersey," said Mr. Baydon. When Mr. Groogins said, "Connecticut," I had a mind to ask if he knew a Mr. Tallmadge—the man to whom Mr. Townsend reported information—but thought better of it.

Once I asked, "Under whom does your commander, this Colonel Livingston, serve?"

"General Arnold."

Dear God! Was coming here the worst thing to have done? But there was no turning away.

On we went until Mr. Baydon said, "Almost there."

Within moments, we stepped out of the forest into a clearing where there were many tree stumps. We proceeded up a small hill. At the hill's crown was a wall of upright logs. Behind that were higher mounds of earth. Perhaps thirty soldiers were standing atop these mounds, muskets in hand. All watched us draw close.

"Fort Lafayette," said Mr. Groogins.

Off to the left I could see the broad expanse of Hudson's River. We had been walking parallel to it all along.

Mr. Baydon lifted his musket over his head and called something. In moments a wide gate in the log wall swung out and we walked into Fort Lafayette.

The fort consisted of an open parade ground enclosed by walls of logs and earth, upon which a few cannons were mounted. All pointed toward the river. Close by, shot was stacked.

In the center of the fort area was a small log house. My escorts led me straight to it and rapped on the door. I looked back. The fort gates had been shut. I would not be able to leave.

"Enter!" called a voice.

We stepped inside the cabin, which was no more than a rayless, musty room with a dirt floor and an unmade cot against one wall. In the center was a table, upon which lay maps, torn and curled at their edges. Seated behind the table was a soldier. As we came forward, he looked up.

A lean, unshaven face with tired, red-rimmed eyes looked upon me with puzzlement. His uniform was dirty, sweat stained. A shock of gray hair suggested he might have been grandfather to the soldiers who had brought me. Though I supposed this man was Colonel Livingston, the fort's commander, I saw nothing officer-like about him. Of course, I had not seen an American officer for three years. This man appeared ordinary, without the military authority or bearing of the British officers I had come to know.

Nonetheless, Mr. Baydon saluted, then told Livingston what I had told them when we met by the side of the river—about the *Vulture* bringing a spy. As the soldier talked, the colonel turned his eyes on me, his expression one of grave suspicion.

"Thank you," he said when Mr. Baydon had done. "Leave us,"

My protectors—as I thought them—saluted and left.

Once they had gone, Colonel Livingston sat back in his chair and studied me in silence, as if trying to connect what Mr. Baydon told him with my person. I could hardly doubt him: me, a wild-looking girl, stepping out of the wilderness proclaiming that someone was about to spy.

For myself, although I had arrived at that part of my plan that required me to tell someone what I knew, I was filled with deep misgivings. Would this man believe me? Those soldiers had treated me as daft. How could this man not do the same? I almost thought so myself.

Moreover, this officer served under Arnold. Was he likely to believe my full tale, that his superior, the great hero, General Benedict Arnold, was about to commit the treason of giving West Point to the British!

In haste, I decided that I would tell him only what was credible and easy to confirm.

"Now, then," he said, "in your own words, tell me what this is about."

"My name is Molly Saville, sir," I said. "I have been working in New York City. At the Kennedy house. General Clinton's headquarters."

When his eyes widened slightly, I supposed I made some impression. He said, "How did you get here?"

"An old couple—a fisherman and his wife—took me partway up the river in their boat. The rest I walked."

"Why did you come?"

"At British headquarters, sir, I overheard that the British were going to send a ship up Hudson's River. That there would be someone on board who intended to spy upon West Point."

"Do you know the name of the ship?"

"The *Vulture*."

"There is such a ship," Colonel Livingston acknowledged. "She patrols the river, watching us."

I waited.

"And you are sure this spy has been sent here from British headquarters in New York City. Where you worked."

"Yes, sir."

"Who did you hear talk about this?"

"A major. Major John André."

He grimaced in such a way that I felt I had gained some more believability. "I know the name," he acknowledged. "Chief of staff under General Clinton. What made you come?"

"Sir, I know the enemy well. I . . . lost my brother. A soldier. To the prison ships. He was taken at Fort Washington."

Livingston nodded, as if that was an acceptable explanation. But then he fussed about his maps, as if uncertain what to do. At length he faced me. "You say you heard all this where you worked. Why were you there?"

"I must live."

"Did my soldiers, the one who just brought you, see the ship?"

"I begged them to look, sir, but they chose not to. Sir, I believe that the spy is going ashore. Or maybe he already has gone. He must be prevented. It's a terrible thing—"

Colonel Livingston cut me off with a wave of his hand. Then he made a show of studying his maps, even drumming his fingers on one of them. As if coming to a decision, he stood up, revealing himself a larger man than I had thought. "You'll need to wait here," he said. "Are you hungry?"

"But—"

"Answer my question, girl!" he barked.

I winced. "Yes, sir," I whispered.

"I'll send some food. Someone will be at the door. No one will bother you. Don't try to leave."

"Yes, sir."

The colonel left me.

Standing alone in that little room, I was all too aware that I had, only to a small degree, achieved what I had wanted; to tell someone enough to prevent the treason. Nonetheless, I had to acknowledge that perhaps I had revealed too little, too late. Perhaps the treason had already happened.

I looked at the maps that lay before me. They were much like the ones in André's office. The same world, different eyes. When I examined them, I was able to determine where I was, a place where the river narrowed. Farther north, on the opposite shore, was a place called Kings Ferry. West Point lay some ten miles farther. On the eastern side, northward, was a village marked as Peekskill. To the south, the closest town was Tarrytown. I knew nothing of these places, save, after a fashion, Tarrytown. Wasn't that where John Paulding resided?

But what did geography matter? I was locked in a room that was all but a prison. Exhausted and frustrated, I sat down on the edge of the bed and almost burst into tears. In haste, I dried my eyes. I must, I told myself, show strength, or they would never believe me.

A soldier brought bread, water, and a piece of dried meat, which, though hard to chew, I ate greedily. I wanted to lay upon the cot, but thought it improper. Instead, I sat back against the wall and waited, wondering how much time we had—if any—to save America. Was that absurd? So be it. I was sure it was true.

Aboard the *Vulture*, André paced the deck restlessly, waiting for the man who would bring him to Arnold.

By the time Colonel Livingston reappeared, I was sitting in complete darkness. Lit lantern in hand, he stood by the open door and studied me as if still perplexed. I stood up and waited for him to speak. "I have sent out some men," he finally said, "to see what the *Vulture* is doing."

"Sir," I replied, "I told you what she's doing."

"You have walked here, miss, out of the wilderness to present me with extraordinary claims."

It was exactly as I feared he would think.

He went on. "I can't act just because you say so. I have to determine for myself. If necessary, I can take action on my own. My commander, General Arnold—"

"Sir!"

"Rest assured, miss, if something were seriously amiss, I would of course inform him."

Not daring to say that Arnold was the *one* person who should not be informed, I said, "When might you do something?"

His only reply was "You may use that cot to sleep."

"But, sir—"

"Good night, miss. Don't try to leave. You will be stopped."

With that, he left me.

I felt defeated, but relieved I had not informed him about General Arnold's treason. That, I am sure, would have made things worse. As if things could be worse than they were.

❖ 59 ❖

ON THE MORNING of September the twenty-second, I awoke wondering what, if anything, had transpired during the night. There was nothing to do but wait and worry.

Do not think I failed to note the date: four years to the same day when I had witnessed Captain Hale's death. That mournful recollection in turn flooded me with painful memories of William's death with all its attending horrors. How many had suffered in this war! And I was doing nothing but sitting in a grimy hut, helpless to do anything. War makes prisoners of everyone.

At length the door opened and a soldier brought in bread and a pitcher of milk. It was a comfort to have it.

Shortly thereafter Colonel Livingston came in. He stood at the door, hand upon the doorjamb, as though reluctant to come near. "I'm sending a troop of soldiers to Tellers Point to watch the *Vulture*," he said. "Regardless of what you say, I don't like her anchored there."

"Has she ever done so before?"

He shook his head. But clearly he was not going to act because a *girl* urged him to. No, he must have his *own* reason to act. As for me, more than anything I wanted to know if John André was still on that ship. After so much had happened, I had the right to learn how things stood.

I said, "Please, sir. I must go with them."

Distrust filled his face. "Why?"

"I want to see if I was right."

"You are a singular young lady. How old are you?"

I lifted my chin. "Fifteen."

"Do you have parents?"

"Yes."

"Do they know what you have done?"

"No, sir. Do you have children?"

"A daughter your age."

"Would you not trust her?" I said, trying to keep my gaze level.

He sighed. "It's a lengthy way to Tellers Point."

"No further than I've already come."

"You'll be under guard."

I said, "You don't believe me, do you?"

He shifted uneasily on his feet, then said, "These are fragile times, miss. You must know how unusual your tale is. It's hard to know what to make of you."

"Do you think me mad?" I said.

He gave no answer.

I said, "Please, I need to go."

He waited a few moments, made a dumb show of reluctance, but then said, "Very well." Madness has its rewards: I think he wished to be rid of me.

I stepped out onto the parade ground. Some seven

soldiers were standing about two cannons mounted on large wheels. As I would learn, one was what they called a six-pounder, which meant it could fire a six-pound weight. The other was a howitzer.

There was also a wagon, in which cannonballs, bags of powder, and shovels were placed. Three horses were to pull all this weight.

Colonel Livingston conferred with Mr. Baydon, who kept glancing at me doubtfully as they talked.

Mr. Baydon broke away and shouted out an order. The small troop of soldiers, horses, cannons, and wagon began to move out along the same path by which I had come. Without waiting for an invitation, I walked behind them, like some camp follower.

Not only were the soldiers quite young, they did not appear to know what to make of my presence. Occasionally there were stolen glances, but none would talk to me.

At one point, I went up to Mr. Baydon. "If the ship is still there," I said, "what will you do?"

"Watch her."

"Nothing more?"

He shrugged. "We shall see."

"Then why have you brought cannons?"

"I have my orders, miss."

It was perfectly obvious that I was being ordered to ask no more questions.

On board the *Vulture*, André and Robinson remained in their cabin. They must have talked about the war, about the future beyond the war. Repeatedly they speculated why Arnold had not appeared. They played cards. They tried to sleep. At one point, Captain Sutherland urged they sail back downriver. André, wishing to wait, informed the captain that he did not feel well and would prefer to remain motionless. The captain agreed.

At Joshua Smith's house, Mr. Smith had brought two of his tenants, the Cahoon brothers, to General Arnold. The general tried to persuade them to row Smith to the *Vulture* that night. The brothers raised objections. Why were they going to a British ship? Why at night? It would be hard work. The only boat they had was large and heavy. It all made them uneasy.

At first Arnold tried to reason with them. Then he offered to pay them a high fee. When they refused, he ordered them to do so as a general. When they still declined, he threatened arrest if they did not do as he required.

The brothers finally agreed. They would pick up Smith at the river's edge at about ten that night, take him to the waiting ship, and bring this Mr. Anderson to shore for a meeting. Afterward, they would get him to the ship.

"One other thing," said Arnold as the brothers started to go.

They paused.

"You will muffle your oars."

As they went off, one of the brothers muttered to the other, "I don't like this business."

It took much time for us to reach Tellers Point. The cannons were heavy, and the pathway, which had been easy to walk, was rough for our transport. Though the horses labored, there were places where the soldiers had to get behind the cannons and push. They even let me help. It was the same for the wagon that carried the cannonballs and shot. In the event, we did not reach Tellers Point until late afternoon. Dusk was with us.

Tellers Point proved to be exactly that, a fat finger of land—a forested peninsula—that extended almost halfway across Hudson's River. Not far from the actual point rose a small hill.

Mr. Baydon, in command, left the cannons behind the hill—that they might be hidden from view—and went to the top. Two other soldiers went with him. I did the same. At the summit, we lay down, so as not to be observed. By then nothing I did seemed to shock them anymore.

Not far from where we were was the actual tip of Tellers Point. Beyond, on the river, the *Vulture* was anchored.

"That spot," said Mr. Baydon, pointing to the very end of Tellers Point, "is what folks call Gallows Point."

His words made me cringe. "Where's West Point?" I asked.

"Ten miles up."

"Might the ship go there?"

"There's a chain across the river to block any passage. Besides, before you would reach it, they would have to get past Fort Lafayette." He nodded toward the *Vulture*. "I suspect she'll stay right here."

"What do you intend to do?" I wanted to know.

"We'll watch her. See if, like you claim, they put someone ashore."

"It might already have happened."

Ignoring me, Mr. Baydon had a telescope, which he put it to his eye.

"Can you see anything?" I asked.

He handed me the device and I peered though it. In the twilight gloom, I saw one, then two, men pacing upon her deck. It was queer to think that one of them might be André. I did wish it. Even so, I reminded myself he might have already gone to his meeting.

As the sky grew dark, a half-moon rose, now and again veiled by clouds. Stars were bright. All was as still as stone. The two men on the *Vulture* paced the deck.

I watched and waited.

At about eleven o'clock, at the foot of Long Clove Mountain, at the southern end of Haverstraw Bay, Joshua Smith came down to the river's edge. In his pocket was a note that allowed Mr. Anderson to pass through American lines. It was written and signed by Arnold.

Sam and Joe Cahoon were waiting in their boat, the blades of their oars wrapped in sheepskins. When Smith appeared, the brothers murmured only a sullen greeting. Mr. Smith stepped into the boat and fixed a small white flag to the bow.

"What's that for?" demanded one of the brothers.

"So we're not shot at."

The men swore. "That likely?" one of them asked.

"No."

The brothers pushed off and began to row. "Where to?" said one of the rowers.

"As you've been told. Tellers Point. There's a ship waiting."

Using the tiller, Mr. Smith steered. Their passage was made easier with the tide running south.

The *Vulture* lay some miles below.

60

I WAS ASLEEP at the bottom of Tellers Point hill when I was awoken by an excited cry. "Mr. Baydon! There's movement."

Mr. Baydon rose instantly and began to run up the hill, following the soldier who had called him. I scrambled along.

Upon reaching the top of the hill, we looked out. Above, clouds were scudding so that the moon came and went as if playing a hiding game. When brightest, it cast glistening light upon the river. At first I saw nothing. Then I saw it: a small boat moving silently toward the *Vulture*. She moved like a water bug, in short forward jerks.

Mr. Baydon put his telescope to his eye. After a while he said, "Three people in the boat. White flag in the bow."

I said, "What does the white flag mean?"

"By the rules of war, they are entitled to safe passage."

"Safe passage?" I said.

"We try to follow the rules, miss."

The boat in which Joshua Smith and the Cahoon brothers sat bumped against the hull of the *Vulture*.

Captain Sutherland, who had been alerted to its approach, leaned over the gunnels. "Who's there?" he called down.

"Mr. Smith. For Mr. Anderson."

"Come aboard," called Sutherland.

Mr. Smith plucked up the flag of truce and climbed to the deck. "I have a pass for Mr. Anderson."

The captain took the paper, read it, and then went down to where André and Robinson were waiting. "He's here, sir. He brought a pass, but only for Mr. Anderson."

"Fine," said André. "I'll go alone."

"Are you sure that's wise?" said Robinson.

"It's as planned. And I wouldn't want it otherwise," said André. "Don't worry. I'll be back soon."

"Your uniform, sir," said the captain. "It's rather visible. May I suggest I get you an overcoat to cover it."

"It's best," agreed Robinson.

Impatient to go, André said, "As you wish."

When a coat was fetched, André put it on. It reached down to his boots, had a high collar, and was blue. Nothing of his uniform could be seen save his boots. The captain offered him a plain three-cornered hat, too. André gave his wig to Robinson and set the hat low upon his head.

Robinson saluted and said, "Godspeed."

André went on deck and approached Mr. Smith.

"Mr. Anderson?" said Smith.

"I'm he," said André.

"Very good, sir."

Joshua Smith led the way, climbing down the rope ladder into the waiting boat. André followed and settled into the bow seat. He kept his hat pulled down.

The Cahoon brothers eyed André. One of them nudged the other. "Let's get home," he said.

They pushed away from the *Vulture*, turned the boat upstream, and began to row. The tide, however, was now against them, making it much harder to row. As for the flag of truce, it had been left behind.

Mr. Baydon held the telescope to his eye and watched as the small boat moved out from behind the *Vulture*. "They're leaving," he announced.

I said, "How many in the boat?"

He took his time. "Four."

"You see," I said, elated. "Someone going ashore. I was right!"

Mr. Baydon grunted, lowered his telescope, and handed it to me. I put the telescope to my eye and saw the small boat with the silhouettes of four men. Two were rowing. One sat in the stern, one the bow. I *wanted* the one in the bow to be André. *Wanted* him to know I was close, watching. *What would he think? Would he be frightened of me?* I must confess, I felt a kind of elation.

Then I noticed something. Turning to Mr. Baydon, I said, "There's no more flag of truce. Can we stop them now?"

"The cannons could never find them."

"But you must do something!"

He thought for a moment. "Maybe we can drive the *Vulture* away. Least that boat won't be able to come back—if it tries."

He ran down the hill. "Up! Up!" I heard him cry. "Unlimber the guns."

With the boat going against the tide, the trip back to Long Clove Mountain cove took quite a while. In the humid air, the sweating Cahoon brothers grew ever more irritated. It was almost 2 a.m. when the boat finally touched land. Mr. Smith, at the stern, leaned forward toward André. "He'll be waiting," he said.

André stepped out of the boat and onto the shore. Boulders lay everywhere, but there was moonlight enough to see a crooked path running through them and up into the forest. André glanced back at Mr. Smith. Mr. Smith waved him forward.

André walked on, but halted where the pathway began to lead up. He peered into the gloom. Beneath the shadowy trees, he saw a man standing. He was of middling height, broad shouldered, his big head, even in the shadow, suggesting power.

"Is that you, Mr. Anderson?" called the man.

André said, "Mr. Moore?"

"I am he."

Major André moved up the path to where General Arnold was waiting. They clasped hands.

When André moved up among the trees, Joshua Smith climbed out of the boat. He went up the path a few yards, wanting to make sure Mr. Anderson was gone. No sooner did he get on land than the Cahoon brothers shoved the boat back into the river.

Hearing a splash, Smith spun about. "Where are you going?" he shouted.

"Home!" cried one of the brothers. "We've had enough of this." They began to row.

"You mustn't!" called Smith, but the boat was already moving down-river. Incapable of taking any action, Smith merely watched. With a start, he swung back toward the forest. Mr. Anderson and General Arnold were out of sight. Not sure what to do, Mr. Smith decided it would be unwise to intrude.

The meeting between Major André and General Arnold lasted two hours. The talk was for the most part about West Point, with Arnold instructing André how best to attack the fort, the vulnerable points, the places Arnold had weakened. The general also spoke about his plan to trick George Washington into being captured.

He held out a detailed plan of West Point, marked with all the defenseless points.

André hesitated.

Arnold pressed him. "When you get back to the city, you'll want to be absolutely sure of what I told you. There's much to remember."

André gazed at the papers in Arnold's hand.

"I assure you," urged Arnold, "the plans will make your attack much easier. A quick success will do much for your honor."

André took the papers.

Then the two men began to negotiate how much money Arnold would receive for handing over the fort. He wanted a lot.

At 4 a.m., the meeting was over, with the two men having reached agreement on everything. Arnold walked André down to the water's edge. Only Mr. Smith was waiting.

"Where's the boat?" Arnold demanded.

"Gone."

Upset, André turned to Arnold.

Arnold, struggling not to show concern, said, "You'll have to wait until the morning to get back to the ship."

"Wait where?" André demanded.

After a moment's consideration, Arnold pointed to Mr. Smith. "His house."

A frustrated André turned and gazed down the river. The water looked to be flowing away from him.

Arnold said, "There really is no choice."

The two men rode horses to Joshua Smith's house. As they went along the road, André saw an American soldier standing on guard. He immediately understood what it meant: they had gone out of the neutral zone and into the American lines. He pulled his collar up and his hat down.

Shortly before 5 a.m., they reached the Smith household, where the two men sat down to breakfast.

I thought Mr. Baydon would never get his cannons in place. First, the men had to roll the heavy pieces up to the top of Teller Point hill. There was no path and little light. Rocks, boulders, and soft spaces hindered them. The six-pounder went first. Then the howitzer. Lastly, they brought along the shot and powder wagon.

Then they had to come *down* the hill to the point, an even harder task, lest the heavy cannons escape their grasp and tip over. The horses were of hardly any use.

I kept my eyes on the *Vulture*. She did not move, but remained as still as the warm air. No one went to her or from her. Her deck was deserted. The gray river waters moved sluggishly.

Once the cannons were at the bottom of the hill, Mr. Baydon ordered the soldiers to build earthworks in front of them, protection in case the *Vulture* fired back. After he divided his men into two batteries, the guns were loaded.

By the time all was in place it was early morning. The first light was pale, the air humid. Shreds of mist trailed over the river. All was still.

"Are we ready?" Mr. Baydon called.

"Yes, sir."

"Commence firing."

A glowing spark was brought to the cannon touch-hole. A flash of fire erupted from the muzzle, followed by an explosion. I watched the six-pound cannonball fly through the windless air like a dead bird. It struck the river twenty yards this side of the *Vulture*, sending up a tall spume of water.

Next moment, the howitzer got off its shot. The arc of

its ball lofted higher than the cannon. It too missed the ship, but not by so far.

"Adjust aim!" Baydon commanded.

On the *Vulture*, men were scurrying about her deck.

It took four more shots before our cannonballs struck the *Vulture*. I saw splinters fly first, then heard a dull thud.

The *Vulture* began to fire back. Their shots fell short.

As daylight grew, our cannonballs began to repeatedly hit the ship. Six shots struck her between wind and water. Sails and rigging were torn. Our firing continued.

From behind the *Vulture*, four small boats emerged. They had ropes attached to the ship. Next moment the ship's anchor broke the water's surface. Without wind, the *Vulture* could not move. To take her out of our cannons' range, they were towing her downriver. I did not think that much damage had been done to her. But it was enough to make her move away.

At Mr. Smith's house, André, hearing cannonading from the river, jumped up from the breakfast table. Standing before the front window, he fixed his eyes on the far shore. He could see Tellers Point and the *Vulture* quite well. Even as he watched, there were puffs of smoke, followed by the discharge of cannons. Then he saw the *Vulture* move, hauled downriver by four small boats. He watched, dumbfounded, as the ship disappeared from view.

61

AS THE *VULTURE* moved downriver, out of cannon range, Mr. Baydon and the soldiers gave a cheer.

But I felt balked. *Was* the fourth man I saw in the small boat André? I wanted to think so. If it was, did that mean he *had* met with General Arnold? Was he still on land? If so, what would he do next? As I recalled, the plan was for him to get to the *Vulture*, that he might sail in haste to New York City. There the transport ships, laden with soldiers, were waiting to be transported up Hudson's and then attack. With the *Vulture* gone, surely André—*if* still on land—would try to get to the city.

I turned to Mr. Baydon. "If that spy tries get to New York City and can't go by ship, how would he go?"

He shrugged. "Walk. Horse."

"Are there roads?"

"Of course. But on the western side of the river, there are plenty of American troops to catch someone. Wouldn't be smart to go that way. Then again, he might cross the river and try to get there by way of Connecticut. Wouldn't be easy, either. Lots of our troops are there, too.

"I suppose his best way, the shortest, would be by working his way down—the reverse of what you did—along Hudson's River to the closest British lines."

"Where are they?"

"Above White Plains but below Tarrytown. Somewhere in between. It's always a bit uncertain. The way to get there is like a funnel. Not many choices."

Hearing "Tarrytown," I immediately recalled John Paulding, William's comrade, who lived there. "How far off is that Tarrytown?"

"About the same distance to Fort Lafayette. But south. You said you sailed up Hudson's. You must have gone right by it."

I said, "Do you know a soldier by the name of John Paulding?"

Mr. Baydon shook his head and lost interest in talking to me. Instead, he busied himself working with his men to get the cannons back to the fort.

Alone, I tried to think what I should do. Yes, André, heading for the city, might be traveling on the western side of the river. Or by way of Connecticut. Or not moving anywhere. But if he *was* moving south, the way Mr. Baydon suggested, I must, at the very minimum, make an effort to stop him. Useless, perhaps, but at least I would have tried. I could not rest easy unless I did.

I decided then that I would go to that Tarrytown, the place where Mr. Paulding told me I might find him. Did he not say I could come to him if I had need? If ever the need, it was now, my last chance to stop André from reaching New York City.

When the soldiers were ready to go to Fort Lafayette, I started walking along with them, at least for the length of Tellers Point. When we came to a split in the path, they turned northward.

"Mr. Baydon," I said. "I'm not going with you."

"Where, then?"

"Back home."

"Not intending to walk, are you?"

"I must."

"Not sure you should, miss. Don't know whom you might meet. They call it the neutral ground, but it isn't. Not really. Cowboys or skinners always lurking. I've seen it. The whole area is in a bad way. You can't trust anyone down there."

"I came, didn't I?"

He seemed as mystified by me as ever. "Suppose," he allowed.

I said, "Good-bye. Thank you," then started, not even looking back. I was sure I could feel his eyes on my back.

It did not take me long to reach the Croton River. Once there I searched for the spot where Mr. Baydon and Mr. Groogins had made the crossing. When I found it, I came upon their canoe easily. I dragged it to the river and, albeit clumsily, for I had never paddled such before, got across.

I felt badly that I had removed the canoe from their use, but the situation was too critical for me to give it much thought. Once across the Croton River I turned westward and retraced my steps. Just before I reached

Hudson's River, I discovered a wide, well-worn road that ran south. Certain it would prove far easier passage than along the river's edge, I took it, hoping it would lead me to Tarrytown. And Mr. Paulding. As I went, I forced myself to acknowledge that there was no certainty he would be there. Or, for that matter, André.

◆ 62 ◆

AT MR. SMITH'S HOUSE, General Arnold told André that, as commander of West Point, he needed to go to his upriver headquarters so as not to arouse suspicion. He told the major that he was welcome to wait and see if the *Vulture* reappeared. "But," he advised, "you might have to travel by land."

André struggled not to show distress. "Won't that be dangerous?"

"Not in the least," Arnold assured him.

"How would I go?"

"The closest British lines will be north of White Plains. I promise you, Mr. Smith knows the land and the people hereabouts perfectly. He'll guide you with safety. Even better, I've drawn up a letter—a pass—signed by me that permits John Anderson to go through the lines. You may be sure: my authority is absolute. No possibility of difficulties. Even if you are stopped, my note will get you through." He held out his hand. "I trust to see you soon."

For hours André paced behind the upper windows of Smith's house, watching for the *Vulture*. From time to time he studied the maps and notes about West Point that Arnold had given him. The attack could not fail. If it could begin. But the time passed slowly, and the *Vulture* did not come back.

All that day I walked along the wide, well-trod path. I went through woods, although now and again there were open areas. Off to my right I caught glimpses of Hudson's River, never far. As for the few homes and barns I observed, all were in pitiable condition. The war had indeed swept the area and reduced much to a sad state. Whether it was by the hands of British or American forces, I could not tell. It was only what Mr. Baydon had told me. Since he also cautioned me not to trust anyone, I remained alert for any danger.

It must have been in the afternoon, when I, thirsty and hungry, saw an old house set back from the path. Its roof, missing shingles, sagged like the back of an old horse. Two front windows were covered with something, not glass. The front door leaned out, as if broken. A skinny wisp of smoke rose from its brick chimney.

Wanting to be sure I was going in the right direction, I decided it would be worthwhile to knock. Perhaps I might also get something to eat.

I drew close to the door—not too close—and called a greeting. When no answer came, I repeated myself, louder. I was about to go away when someone, bent and broken, emerged from inside. It took me a moment to realize it was a man.

"Good day, sir," I called.

"Who are you?"

"Please, sir. I need to get to Tarrytown. Is this the way?"

"You British? American?"

"American."

"Someone stole my cow," he let me know, voice heavy with injury.

"Not I, sir. I'm truly sorry for your loss. Is this the way to Tarrytown?" I asked again.

"Seven miles," said the old man with a feeble gesture of his thin hand as he went back into the house.

I didn't ask for food. But at least I was going the right way and it was not far.

Joshua Smith approached André. "Sir, I doubt that ship is going to come back. In any case, even if it does, I have no means of reaching it."

"What do you propose, sir?"

"General Arnold has left a horse for you. And he told me he issued you a pass with his name. That's as good as gold. I assure you, no one among the upper party will challenge it. The east side of the river will be best. I'll take you as far as the Croton River, Pines Bridge. Once there, you'll have no trouble getting south in safety."

André, who must have wondered if Smith knew who he was, only said, "I suppose that's best."

"But you'll have to get out of that uniform, sir," said Smith. "We'll be in American-controlled territory. Civilian clothing will be better. General Arnold asked me to provide some. I'll get them right now. And, sir," said Smith, "if we're to use the ferry at Kings, we'll need to hurry."

In private, André changed out of his uniform. The civilian clothes Smith gave him fit him reasonably well, but he kept his own military boots. As for the maps and papers Arnold had provided—about West Point fortifications—André slipped them in his left sock, pulled the sock on, and stepped into the boot. All was out of sight and secure.

Once dressed, with a wide-brimmed hat firmly on his head, André joined Mr. Smith. He was ready to go.

André mounted a brown horse with a white star on its forehead. On the left shoulder, letters had been branded. They read "USA."

I began to see more houses and farms. These were in better condition than the sad house I had seen previously. It gave me some expectation that I was approaching Tarrytown. The thought revived my strength.

Farther on, I saw Hudson's River on my right. The town must be on its shore. Then I passed an old stone church in good repair. I crossed over a creek, walked on, and saw a school, a blacksmith shop, a few private houses, as well as some people going about their business. I choose an old dame to speak to, who, when I came near her, observed me with such distaste that I needed no mirror to know my deplorable state.

"Good evening, mistress. Can you help me?"

"With what?" she said, backing up a step. I suspect she thought me a beggar.

"Is this Tarrytown?"

"What else would it be?"

"I'm looking for Mr. John Paulding."

"What need do you have of him?" she demanded.

"He's a family friend. I must find him."

She gazed upon me with much severity. "I have no idea where he is," said the woman.

Heart sinking, I took a step away.

"But if he's anywhere near," she called after me, "I suppose it will be at Van Tassel's tavern."

I waited for her to say more.

"Right along there," she said, pointing. Though feeling she was sending me away, I nonetheless went as she directed. As I walked I tried not to think what would happen if I could not find Mr. Paulding.

The tavern, a two-story wooden building, was close. Over the wide door, a swinging sign bore the painted words "Van Tassel." Next to its door was a bench. Sitting there was a portly, bewhiskered man, smoking a clay pipe. A sleeping dog lay at his feet.

Agitated at the thought that Mr. Paulding would not be there, I approached slowly. When the man by the door paid me no mind, I pulled at the heavy door and stepped inside.

- 63 -

IT WAS LATE afternoon when Joshua Smith and John André, on horses, set off along the three-mile roadway north to Kings Ferry. From that point, they hoped to cross Hudson's to its eastern shore. Smith took the lead. André had his coat collar up, his brimmed hat turned low, his eyes on his horse's neck. He and Smith did not speak. The only sound was the *clop-clop* of the horse hooves and the squeaking of saddles.

Unexpectedly they were joined by an American soldier on horseback.

"Mr. Smith," said the soldier. "Good afternoon to you!"

"Ah! Sergeant Michael," said Mr. Smith. "It is good to see you."

"The same," said the soldier, coming alongside Smith. "Heading for the ferry?"

"With my friend Mr. Anderson," said Smith, gesturing. "And you, sir, where are you going?"

"West Point. But it's a pleasant afternoon."

"It is, sir."

As the other two men chatted about the weather, André said nothing.

After a few moments the sergeant said, "Forgive me, gentlemen. I need to hurry. Good evening, sir. Mr. Anderson: A pleasure to meet you." The soldier put his horse to a gallop and was gone.

"There," said Smith. "Easily done."

André made no reply.

A short time later Mr. Smith said, "We're nearing the ferry, sir. Be advised, people might be there."

When I entered Van Tassel's tavern, I stood just within the door and peered into smoke-layered gloom. Lanterns, lit by candles, hung from the ceiling and revealed tables, settles and chairs, and on one wall, a rack of clay pipes, like the man outside had been smoking. A few men were there. Only one of them glanced up at me. It was not Mr. Paulding.

In a far corner of the room was the cagelike enclosure from which drinks were served. Inside of it stood a large barrel of a man. As I stood there looking about, he called, "Who you looking for, girl?"

"Mr. John Paulding, sir."

The man pointed across the room. I turned. In the dim recess of a corner, I saw William's friend. He was seated in a chair smoking a clay pipe. He must have heard his name spoken, for he considered me quizzically. When he did not appeared to recognize me, I took a step in his direction. That was when I realized he was wearing a green coat. It was the kind worn by German troops.

Hesitating, I wondered, had he turned sides?

"Were you looking for me, miss?" he called.

"Mr. Paulding," I said, my voice all a waver. "It's me, Sophia Calderwood. William Calderwood's sister."

He jumped up. "Miss Calderwood? Is that really you?"

"Yes, sir." I took a moment to strengthen myself, but then faced him and said, "You told me if I ever had a need, I could come to you."

Mr. Smith and André reached a bluff overlooking the Kings Ferry landing. In the dusky twilight, André saw the river and, beyond, the eastern shore. The river was narrow here, a good place for a ferry to be working. Midstream, a flat boat was approaching with six men, three on either side, wielding oars. Amidships, a man in civilian clothing stood by a horse.

On the western side were four mounted soldiers in the blue-and-buff uniforms of the American army. They appeared to be waiting for the ferry to land. Smith urged his horse down the incline. André followed. The American soldiers, hearing horses, turned and watched them approach.

Mr. Smith called out, "Captain Miller, sir. A good evening to you!"

"To you, too, Mr. Smith, sir," said the soldier. He touched fingers to his hat.

"Crossing over?" asked Smith.

The soldier nodded toward the incoming ferry. "Waiting for a Frenchman. An engineer to work upon the river chain. And you, sir?"

"Going over. Escorting a commercial friend of General Arnold." He gestured to André. "Mr. Anderson."

The soldiers shifted in their saddles. It was Captain Miller who said, "A good evening to you, sir."

André nodded but did not speak.

The ferry reached the shore. The man who was leading the horse stepped off and was greeted by the American soldiers. After a few remarks, and brief farewell words to Mr. Smith, the five men headed north.

André and Smith, saying nothing, dismounted and led their horses onto the ferry. Smith handed one of the boatmen some paper money. The rowers gathered up their oars. As André and Smith held their horses' bridles, the boat began to cross back over Hudson's.

"That's Verplanck's Point," said Smith, indicating the far side. "Just beyond is a fort. Fort Lafayette. We'll need to make a courtesy stop."

"Why?"

"These people all know me," said Smith, keeping his voice low. "It will appear more natural and ordinary if we stop."

When they reached the far side, Smith and André led their horses off the ferry and remounted.

"The fort is right over there," said Smith. "It won't be a problem, sir. Colonel Livingston commands. I assure you, he and I know each other well."

John Paulding pulled out his chair and begged me to sit, which I was grateful to do. Putting aside his pipe, he dragged over a bench and straddled it, facing me. "What has happened? Why are you here?"

I was so relieved to be with my friend, I simply sat there, hands in my lap, unable to speak or look at him.

"Are you hungry? Can I get you something to drink?"

When all I could do was nod, he fetched me bread, meat, and something to drink, which I took as if I were famished. In truth, I was. Then he again sat and faced me, but remained quiet. Only when I had eaten enough to calm myself, I said, "Thank you. I'm much better now."

He repeated his questions.

Deeply grateful to have found a friend, and so worn with all that had happened, I told Mr. Paulding *everything*. Well, perhaps not all. I spoke of William's death three years ago and how I vowed I would avenge it. I did *not* tell him that I believed Major André could have saved my brother's life. But I revealed my spy work with Mr. Townsend, though I was careful not to reveal his name. Finally I explained in detail all I had learned at the British headquarters regarding Major André and General Arnold's plot. I told him of André's plan to meet Arnold. The role the *Vulture* played. I related how I got to Fort Lafayette, how the officer there, Colonel Livingston, sent a squad of soldiers with cannons to drive the boat away, which it did.

At my continual revelations, Mr. Paulding was nothing less than astonished. "Are you sure of this? General Arnold? You've no doubts about this treason?"

"None."

"But—"

"I assure you, Mr. Paulding"—I was pleading now—"I know General Arnold's high reputation. He was my hero too. But I know what he intends to now do—or may have already done. From what I saw," I said, "I'm fairly certain that Major André got off the ship and went to meet Arnold somewhere. We drove the *Vulture* away, so if the major intends to go back to the city—and I think he must—there is a good chance he will pass through this area."

"And if he doesn't come this way?"

"Then I can do nothing. And West Point will be lost."

Mr. Paulding was silent for a moment before he said, "We need to inform someone in command. I report to a Colonel Jameson. A Virginia man."

I said, "No one has been willing to believe me."

When he said nothing—suggesting that he too did not think what I said was true—I went on. "Mr. Paulding, I know the affection you have for my family, and my brother. I presume you care for me, too. But you don't believe me either, do you?"

He had the kindness not to admit it. Rather, he rubbed his face and hair with a hand, as if to work all the information I'd given him into his brain. I made myself sit there, eyes full of feeling. As he gazed upon my face, I had the sensation he was seeking some shade, some glimmer of his friend William, as if that would reassure him. And indeed, he finally said, "What do you want me to do, Miss Calderwood?"

"Mr. Paulding," I fairly wept, "if Major André comes this way, we must stop him. If he reaches the city, it will be a calamity. General Clinton—with a host of troops—is waiting for him there to seize West Point. The war will be lost."

✦ 64 ✦

MAJOR ANDRÉ, GUIDED by Mr. Smith, moved away from Kings Ferry. Almost immediately, they made a turn and came upon a clearing. Looking up a small hill, André saw what he assumed was Fort Lafayette. A soldier was standing on guard over the gate.

As Mr. Smith approached, he lifted a hand. "Mr. Joshua Smith!" he called out. "Compliments to Colonel Livingston." He turned in his saddle, then shouted at the guard. "General Arnold's good friend. Mr. Anderson."

In moments, the gate swung open.

When the two horses trotted into the fort, the gate closed behind them. From the small building in the center of the parade ground, Colonel Livingston stepped out.

"Mr. Smith!" he called "A good evening to you, sir."

"And to you, sir," said Smith. "General Arnold's friend Mr. Anderson."

"Sir," said Livingston, greeting André with a nod. To Smith he said, "I was about to sit down for dinner. May I interest you gentlemen?"

"I'm afraid we must get on to Peekskill," said Smith.

"Just paying my compliments before moving on."

"Will you be seeing General Arnold soon?" Livingston asked Smith.

"In a day or two, I should think."

"Would you deliver a letter to him? We had some small action this morning. He should know about it."

"Most willing to oblige," said Smith. "Was the action serious?"

"We drove away a British ship," called Livingston as he walked to his cabin. "Nothing too important." Within moments, he came back with a letter, which he handed up to Smith. "Much obliged, sir."

"My pleasure. Good evening."

André nodded.

With Smith still in the lead, the two men left the fort and proceeded north. As they trotted along, Mr. Smith said, "The road isn't simple. After four miles north, we'll turn east, and only then south. Once you get to Pines Bridge, you'll be fine."

As the twilight thickened, they began to canter, but just before they reached Peekskill, Smith turned east along a winding, hilly way. It was after going another two miles that they observed a group of men blocking the road. By the light of the lanterns these men carried, it was easy to see that they were armed.

At the same moment, in Tarrytown, Mr. Paulding said, "Very well, Miss Calderwood, if your man comes this way, I will try and stop him. But we may not be able to.

As you have suggested, there are any number of ways such a man could pass south. Where did you last see him?"

"I'm guessing he was on the western side of Hudson's. North of Tellers Point."

"What makes you think he'd come back to this shore?"

"One of the American soldiers from Fort Lafayette told me the closest British lines were at a place called White Plains. To reach it he would most likely come this way."

Mr. Paulding seemed doubtful. "How much," he said, "of this plot did you tell Colonel Livingston?"

Not only did I feel close to tears, I found it hard to breathe. "Mr. Paulding," I confessed, "I was sure he wouldn't believe me, so I told him just a small amount. His commander is Arnold. What if Livingston told him what I said? In the end, the colonel insisted upon finding his own reasons to drive away the ship."

I had no doubt Mr. Paulding was finding my story too fantastical, for he became very silent. At length he said, "But you are quite certain the man will come this way?"

"No!" I cried. "I am *not* certain. I was merely told the Jersey side has many of our soldiers. The same for Connecticut. That it would be hard for Major André to get through those places. That this was his most likely route."

"True," said Mr. Paulding. "And if he does come this

way—and you agree, we don't know if he will—most likely he'll aim for Dobbs Ferry. It's neutral ground. Not too far beyond is White Plains, as you say, the nearest British lines. Get there and he's free.

"Now, *if* he does go from where you think he was, he'll need to cross over at Kings Ferry, then travel south by Pines Bridge. Mind, after that bridge, there are *two* roads coming south. One goes through North Castle, where there is an American army post. That's where my Colonel Jameson is in command with a squad of dragoons. If your André learns about that—and let's hope he does—more than likely he will avoid it. As for the other road, it does lead here. So—if you are right—*if*," he repeated, "there is a chance he will come this way."

How I hated the word "if."

"Mr. Paulding," I pleaded, "I know you only—at best—half believe me. While *I* know what I say is happening, I beg you, not for my sake, but for William's, for all those murdered prisoners, will you try to stop the major?"

"I'll be honest with you, Miss Calderwood. Your story about General Arnold *is* beyond belief." He scratched an ear. "I don't like to believe you. I don't wish to. But seeing it's you, and in William's honor, I'm willing to try what you ask. That said, I don't see the point of sharing what you claim. You're right. Not many will find your story convincing. They'll ask for proof. You can't give any, can you?"

I shook my head.

"Never mind, I have friends who'll follow me. We'll

post ourselves on the road and see what happens. But it can't be till the morning."

"Mr. Paulding—"

"It's the best I can do."

Seeing the armed men, Mr. Smith reined in his horse.

"May I suggest," Mr. Smith said to André in a low voice, "you have your pass from General Arnold ready."

"Friends!" shouted Mr. Smith, and they moved forward.

One of the armed men stepped forward. "Gentlemen," he announced. "Captain Ebenezer Boyd at your service. Third Westchester Militia. What business brings you here?"

"On behalf of General Arnold," said Smith, gesturing to André. "Mr. Anderson. A friend of the general. I'm guiding him south."

Without waiting for a request or speaking, André leaned down and handed the militiaman Arnold's pass. While one of the soldiers held up a lantern, Captain Boyd read it. Once, twice, he gazed up at André, as if to connect him with what was written.

"Very good, sir," said Boyd, making something of a salute, and then handing the letter back to André. "You may pass. But be advised, gentlemen, there are plenty of the lower party about. I suggest you put up for the night, somewhere near. There's Tucker's place just along. Tell him I suggested he take you in."

"Thank you, sir," said Smith.

André touched his horse's flanks with his heels. He and Smith passed on.

"He was right," said Smith after they had gone a while. "It's too dark to go on with safety. We'll need to find a place to sleep."

They passed a house with candlelight in a window.

"We'd better stop here," said Smith.

John Paulding stood up. "We'll need to find you a place to sleep," he said to me. "And, if I may suggest it, perhaps some better clothing."

I felt a need to say, "May I ask about your coat?"

"My Hessian coat?" He laughed. "That time I saw you in New York, and after I saw my intended, I was picked up by the night watch and thrown into the sugarhouse. Remember how you told me William said it took strength to escape? I decided to make a try while I still had some. Once out, I relieved a soldier of his coat. German coats are very fine." He grinned. "The spoils of war."

I followed him out of the tavern. Once outside, he paused, as if deciding where to go. "This way," he announced.

There were houses with lamps to allow us to make our way along a street that looped toward the river. As we walked along, I could see something of Tarrytown, with its fair number of houses.

Mr. Paulding approached one of them. I stayed close. When he knocked on the door, an elderly woman, holding a candlestick, looked out.

"Mrs. Abbatt," said Paulding in greeting. "John Paulding."

"Ah! Mr. Paulding," said the woman. "Good evening." But upon seeing me, her face squeezed as if she just tasted raw lemon.

"A favor, Mrs. Abbatt," said Mr. Paulding. "This is Miss Sophia Calderwood. Her family are close friends of mine. She needed to flee the city, and came to me for help. A bed to sleep tonight is humbly requested. Would you be kind and accommodate her?"

Mrs. Abbatt considered me with more sympathetic eyes. "She does look weary."

"Walked all the way," said Paulding.

"Goodness," said the woman, her face softening further. "Come in, child."

"Mrs. Abbatt, my many thanks. Miss Calderwood, I'll come for you early."

I turned to thank Mr. Paulding, but he was already gone.

Mrs. Abbatt proved kind, first giving me a bucket and cloth to wash myself. Then she insisted I change out of my by now ragged and filthy clothing. What she gave me was hardly fashionable, but no dress could ever be more warmly received. Moreover, she was civil enough to ask no questions.

When she guided me to a private bed, I fairly fell into it. Even so, I lay there wide awake with the realization that the next day would bring success or horrible failure.

Mr. Smith approached the house. In such light as there was, André could see it was a run-down structure.

Smith knocked upon the door. It took some time and a few more knocks before the door opened. An old man holding up a glowing lantern peeked out.

"Yes?"

"Mr. Tucker? Joshua Smith at your service, sir. On business for General Arnold. My companion Mr. Anderson. I'm afraid night has overtaken us. Captain Boyd, just down the road, suggested you might be willing to put up a couple of weary travelers."

The man examined Smith, then André.

"We have papers from the general to prove our peaceful mission," said Smith.

"General Arnold? All right, then," said the man. "Mind! I've but one spare room and bed."

"Much obliged," said Smith.

André and Smith, both wrapped in their coats, shared the bed. André didn't even bother to take off his boots.

"How much further will I need to go?" he asked.

"You'll be in the city tomorrow," said Smith. "With ease."

As André tried to sleep, all he could think was that in twenty-four hours, he would be safe and triumphant.

❖ 65 ❖

MR. SMITH AND Major André were up at dawn. They thanked the man who had put them up for the night. André offered to pay something, but was refused, with the words, "You can pass the welcome on to others in good time."

When the two men mounted their horses, the light of dawn was made dimmer with a morning fog and slight drizzle.

"Don't worry," said Mr. Smith. "I know the road perfectly. We're heading for the town of Crompond."

They moved slowly through the fog.

It was Mrs. Abbatt, who, with a gentle shake of my shoulder, woke me from deep sleep.

"Your friend Mr. Paulding is here," she said. "He's waiting in the kitchen."

Though my body sorely ached, I bestirred myself. The morning's light was dullish. The air felt damp. I went into the kitchen, where Mr. Paulding was waiting. He seemed to fill the small room's space.

"Good morning, Miss Calderwood," he said. "I have

managed to find some friends to help us."

Mrs. Abbatt handed me a bowl of warm milk and some bread. I devoured it in haste and handed her back the bowl. "Thank you for your kindness, madam," I said.

"My pleasure. I hope all goes well."

So did I.

John Paulding and I stepped out of the house. A thin ground fog and slight drizzle softened the world much like the fuzz upon a peach. Two young men were waiting. Each had muskets in the crooks of their arms.

"My friends," said Mr. Paulding, introducing them. "Isaac Van Wart. David Williams. Gentlemen, my family friend Miss Calderwood."

They nodded friendly greeting, but said no words.

"We need to wait along the Albany Road," Mr. Paulding explained. "Do you mind the wet?" he said to me.

"Not at all."

"We'd best go on."

We left the town and turned north along the same road I had come by the day before. Mr. Paulding's friends went before us.

"Mr. Paulding—" I said. "If we do stop Major André, what will happen next?"

"I'll be honest and say I hadn't thought that far ahead. But I suppose we'd turn him over to the regular army."

"What will they do with him?"

"If what you say is correct, I suppose they'll hang him."

I felt as if someone had struck me across the face.

Let it be admitted, throughout my pursuit of John André I had never contemplated what might be the consequence if he were captured. All my efforts had been on preventing his meeting with General Arnold and then averting the loss of West Point. Yet despite those efforts, evidence suggested—but did not yet prove—that a meeting *had* taken place. In short, as far as I knew, I had failed.

The one chance of stopping the treasonous play was to keep André from reaching New York City. Now, perhaps, with Mr. Paulding's help, we could stop him. But if we did, and Mr. Paulding did turn him over to our regular soldiers, what did I wish to happen next?

I will say it plain: the mere consideration that John André might be *hung* appalled me. I beg you to recall that I had never forgotten Nathan Hale and his fate. The notion of André being hung filled me with profound horror. And guilt.

Did I feel guilty that I might be the means by which he might die? Or—was I guilty of wishing to spare him?

But—was not John André the enemy? Did he not refuse to help William and therefore bring on my brother's ghastly death? Had I so forgotten the nightmare of the sugarhouse and the *Good Intent*? Had John André not taken up arms and used them to kill my countrymen? On the field of battle? In prisons? Was not his government, his king, bent upon suppressing our freedom, our natural rights? Was he not at this same moment working to bring defeat to my country?

He was guilty of those things.

Were these not reasons enough to stop him?

Was I to be that gross and false image, the *weak* woman, who pushes aside all *reason* to embrace the folly of blind emotion?

The mere possibility was a scandal to me, Sophia Calderwood, who wished to think of myself as strong of will and mind. John André no longer knew me. Why should I know him as other than the enemy?

And yet I was anguished, an anguish from which I could not free myself.

I have said before how the war made us live lives of deception. There was the question, had I deceived *myself*? Was all I'd done for a noble cause, to have my nation's fair revenge? Or were my actions motivated by my wish for him to recognize *me*? To treat me as he had done when I was a girl? When I fancied he cared for me?

How contemptible! How low! How degrading!

Never mind what I been. The question was, what would I do . . . now?

The fog had mostly lifted when John André and Joshua Smith, moving south, reached the small cluster of houses known as the town of Crompond. Blocking the road was an armed young man in American uniform.

"Captain Foote!" he announced himself. "Where are you men going?"

"General Arnold asked me to escort Mr. Anderson south," replied Mr. Smith.

André handed down Arnold's pass. Captain Foote

glanced at it briefly, handed it back, and waved them on. "Colonel Jameson's dragoons are at Wright's Mill," he said to André. "They might give you an escort."

Mr. Smith thanked the young officer. He and André headed south. "Sounds like you might want to avoid Wright's Mill," said Mr. Smith.

André heard the warning but said nothing.

They stopped at a farmhouse and asked an old woman if they could buy some food. The woman offered some corn mush, which was gratefully received. She would not take an offered payment.

A mile farther down the road Mr. Smith halted. "Well, sir," he said. "Pines Bridge is just a short way along. From here on, you'll more likely find less Continental troops and more cowboys. You know, those of the lower party. To be honest, I've worked to keep myself in the shade—neither light or dark. You'd best go on yourself."

"I'm sure I'll be fine," said André, and the two shook hands. "Thank you for all your efforts, sir."

With a farewell wave, Smith turned his horse and headed back north. André, now alone, pressed toward the south. When he reached the Croton River, he passed over the Pines Bridge. Half a mile farther on, he came upon a boy walking by the road.

"Hello, lad. Am I heading right for Wright's Mill?"

" 'Bout a mile on there's a fork. To the left for Wright's Mill. To the right for Tarrytown."

"Thank you," said André, and threw the boy a six-pence for his information.

André pressed on. As the boy had told him, he reached a fork in the road. He paused. Wright's Mill was where the American dragoons were stationed. He turned to the right, toward Tarrytown.

⋆ 66 ⋆

WITH MR. PAULDING in the lead, the three men moved along the road. I came behind, trying desperately to deal with my swirling thoughts and emotions. *What have I done?* I kept asking myself. *What should I do?*

Shortly after we left town, Mr. Pauling brought us to a thickly wooded area that crowded in upon both sides of the road.

"Miss Calderwood," said Mr. Paulding. "My friends and I shall keep ourselves on this side. I suggest you remain on the other side, out of sight. But not so far that I can't signal to you. If someone appears, I'll look to you. You'll need to watch. If it's your man, just raise your hand and we'll stop him. If you don't signal, we'll let him pass on. Does that make sense?"

"Yes, sir," I replied, finding it hard to speak. "It does."

"Do you wish to confront him?"

"No," I said instantly.

We deployed ourselves. The three of them went to one side of the road, and I, quite alone, was fairly hidden on the other.

As we waited, all those questions I just laid before

you kept churning within my head, each with a multitude of possibilities, choices, wishes, and regrets. I did not know what to think. Or do.

It all came to two things: What were my feelings about John André? And if he did come, how should I act?

What feelings *did* I have for him?

I believe we waited for a few hours. It was yet morning, and I was still lost in all my mental commotion when I saw that Mr. Paulding was waving his hand at me.

With a pounding heart, I turned my eyes along the road.

A man appeared, pushing a barrow.

When I saw that it was not André, I made no sign to Mr. Paulding. The man passed by. We continued to wait.

It was not long before a brown horse and rider appeared.

Though his clothing was utterly different than I had ever seen upon him, I immediately knew it was John André. What's more, I could tell from the way he sat upon the horse that he was exhausted. And I, my heart anything but calm, felt a pang of pity for the man.

I darted a glance across the road. Mr. Paulding was looking right at me, waiting again for me to sign—or not.

Oh, weak heart, I cried to myself, *tell me what to do! Shall I preserve his life or mine?*

I lifted my hand.

The moment I did, Mr. Paulding and his two friends

fairly leaped out upon the road so that Major André could not go forward. Taken by surprise, he clutched nervously at the horse's reins and stared down upon the men, but mostly at Mr. Paulding, who had grabbed the horse's bridle.

In fact, I believe the green German military coat my friend was wearing confused him. For André, settling himself upon his saddle with all his dignity on display, said, "Gentlemen, I trust you belong to *our* party."

"What party is that?" said Mr. Paulding.

"The lower," said André. Then he added, "I am an officer in the British service and have been on particular business in the country. I hope you will not detain me."

The men exchanged glances, after which Mr. Paulding said, "Climb down, sir."

André, not budging, said, "But I must get along."

No one moved.

"Down, sir!" insisted Paulding.

Apparently grasping that he must deal with these men, André pulled out Arnold's pass and handed it down. Isaac Van Wart took it and unfolded it. I rather suspect he could not read, for he passed it to Mr. Paulding, whom I knew could.

"My lads," said an impatient André, "you're going to get yourselves into a lot of trouble."

Mr. Van Wart grinned and said, "But you just said you were a British officer."

"I'm engaged upon the general's business," said André. "Do you intend to rob me?"

"You need not worry," said Mr. Paulding. "We don't intend to take your money."

"Good," said André. "I don't have any."

"British officers always have money," said Mr. Van Wart. He turned to Mr. Paulding.

"Let's search him," said Paulding.

"Get down," commanded Mr. Williams.

After a moment of hesitation, André dismounted. The men removed his coat and jacket and went through his pockets. They found two watches and a few dollar bills, nothing more. They threw the clothing onto the ground.

"Take off your boots," said Mr. Van Wart.

André looked hard at him—as if insulted by the demand—but sat down upon the ground. Mr. Van Wart bent over and yanked off both boots. The men searched inside them. Once more, they found nothing.

It was Mr. Paulding who said, "Take off your socks."

André did not move, but just sat there. Mr. Williams reached down and yanked off the right sock. They found nothing. It was an impatient Mr. Paulding who pulled off the left sock. When he did, the papers Arnold had given André tumbled out.

Williams snatched them up and handed all to Mr. Paulding, who examined the papers closely. It was then he said, "This man is a spy."

❖ 67 ❖

IN ALL OF these proceedings, Mr. Paulding did not look at me. I am equally certain that John André never noticed me in my place of concealment. Yet I, to my increasing mortification, watched and heard it all. The way the men went through André's pockets, pulled away his boots, and then stripped him of his stockings was like some crude mockery. I have no doubt that for André, it being low Americans who had accosted him and treated him thus was deeply wounding to his pride.

Indeed, the major, standing there in his bare feet, offered the men a large sum of money—a bribe—if they would let him pass. He smiled. He tried his charm. He bullied. He threatened. He offered more money. The three men refused it all. To see André's growing frustration, anger, and finally his humiliation made me ashamed. Had I not tried bribes to free William?

It was Mr. Paulding who said to him, "Mount up. We need to take you to Colonel Jameson. He's my superior. He can decide what to do with you."

André put on his socks and shoes slowly. I knew him well enough to read his thoughts and looks: *How dare such men treat me so!* As if to regain some dignity, he picked up his coat and hat and dusted them off.

Only then did he remount his horse. Once set, he again offered money for his freedom, considerably more than he had before. It was to no avail.

Taking the reins of André's horse in hand, Mr. Williams began to lead the way north, along the road. Mr. Van Wart took a place by André's side, one hand on the major's boot, as if to remind him he was there. Mr. Paulding came last, behind the horse.

As they started off, Mr. Paulding turned to determine where I was.

Wobbly with emotion, I stepped out onto the road. For a moment I stood there and watched them move along, incapable of clear thought. Part of me wished to run away. The greater part insisted that I must see all that happened. And indeed, I did follow, but kept a considerable distance behind. Yes, I did not want John André to see me. I also did not wish the men to see the pain in my heart.

What have I done?

The answer I insisted upon—then—was *I have saved my country.*

· 68 ·

ALONG WITH HIS FRIENDS, Mr. Paulding led John
André in the direction of Wright's Mill. Along the way,
they paused at a place called Reed's Tavern, where
Major André was given milk and bread.

I stood apart and watched him. He seemed despondent. How strange for me to see him without his charm,
his beguiling smiles and graces. It made me think of
a puppet from which the inner, living hand had been
removed, making him empty of life.

It was at Reed's Tavern that Mr. Paulding discovered
that Colonel Jameson and his troops had been transferred to a place called North Castle, some six miles
farther. They turned that way.

When Mr. Paulding informed me of their new direction, he asked me what I wished to do.

"I'll follow along," I said.

As they went, I am quite sure that John André never
so much as glanced back to where I was, for as before
I remained some distance behind. Thus I always was
there, always watching, but never part of the group that
included John André.

Yet, in my way, was I not the closest of all?

I kept asking myself, *What is this man to me?* I kept reminding myself that he had been trying to destroy my country.

As we moved along, Mr. Paulding twice came to inquire after me. I assured him I was fine in all respects, which, of course, was not true. Making no explanations, I told Mr. Paulding I preferred to continue but keep out of sight.

So it was that we walked all day, the only one mounted being André.

Late afternoon we reached North Castle, a place hardly more than a sawmill and a few farmhouses. Here Mr. Paulding found Colonel Jameson and his troop of dragoons. They were awaiting the arrival of some important officer whose name was not mentioned. As soon as we arrived, Mr. Paulding turned Major André— along with the papers they had found on him—over to the colonel.

The news of André's capture and who he was quickly spread among the soldiers and then, apparently, elsewhere. I hardly know how, but soon civilians, attracted by the hubbub, gathered. The word "spy" was on all lips.

When I drew close, no one paid me any mind. No doubt each group thought I was part of another group. You may be sure I never let André see me.

The enthusiasm brought on by who and what André was, and the seriousness of the charge against him, as well as there being no meeting house, was such that a loud discussion about what to do with him was conducted in public.

There was no question about the meaning of the papers found on André—plans and diagrams about an attack on West Point. Colonel Jameson was greatly shocked, as were all the other soldiers on duty. So too the civilians. Yet, let it be noted that General Arnold had not put *his* name on them. Still, there was that pass Arnold had provided for "Mr. Anderson." That *seemed* to incriminate André and Arnold, but it was not conclusive. Then again, the major *had* told Mr. Paulding and his friends that he was a *British officer*. He further claimed, "I'm engaged upon the general's business."

Arnold's role in all this thus remained a mystery to all—save Mr. André and me. I, in my emotional turmoil, was hardly going to step forward and proclaim what I knew. For his part, André was not about to reveal what he had been doing.

There we were, bound together by knowledge neither dared to reveal.

Colonel Jameson made two decisions. First, he decided to send all the captured papers to General George Washington, who was apparently somewhere close, in Connecticut. Second, Jameson made up his mind to send Major André to General Arnold's headquarters. There was some logic in this insofar as Arnold was, after all, the commander of West Point, and Jameson's superior. Jameson believed it was General Arnold's responsibility to deal with this presumed spy.

Mr. Paulding objected. When pressed for a reason,

he, unwilling to engage me, and reluctant to accuse Arnold, could give no reason. In so doing, he was easily overruled by his superior, Colonel Jameson.

To be sure, André made no protest. He must have been aware that being sent to Arnold was the best thing that could happen to him.

With intense perplexity, I watched and listened but did nothing when the major, arms tied behind his back, and guarded by a lieutenant and four militiamen, was taken away. To Arnold!

I was of two minds. I was relieved that no *personal* harm would come to André, at least no harm by *my* hand. West Point, I told myself, could still be saved and Arnold exposed. It was everything I desired.

However, when Colonel Jameson chose to send André to General Arnold, I had no doubt that Arnold would protect him. Worse, it was more than likely that Arnold would find a way to free André to do as much destruction as the two had always planned. Arnold's traitorous designs might remain hidden. The loss of West Point might still take place.

In short, once again, all I had done was in jeopardy.

When André was led away, Mr. Paulding came to me and offered to guide me back to Tarrytown.

"Mr. Paulding," I said, "remember what I told you about General Arnold. It's a great mistake to send André to him."

"There was nothing I could do, Miss Calderwood. You have no proof."

It was then—as if Providence again chose to take

things in hand—that into North Castle rode Major Benjamin Tallmadge. With his arrival, everything changed. Again.

Who was Major Tallmadge?

Nothing makes me remember a fact more than being told to unknow it, and Tallmadge was the name Mr. Townsend had urged me to blot from memory—the man to whom he passed on the information I gave him.

And here was Major Tallmadge in New Castle.

Colonel Jameson, his superior, told him all that had happened. The major was upset. "Was it wise to send that man to Arnold?" he demanded.

"What objections could you possibly have?" asked Jameson.

"Why did Arnold give that British major a pass?" Tallmadge asked. "Why did he say he was on business with the general?"

Jameson had no answer.

Tallmadge, greatly troubled, took himself off, as if he had a need to think what to do. I observed him, as he stood slouched against a tree, falling into what is called a "brown study," some gloomy meditation.

Convinced that Providence was again supplying me the chance to stop the harm I had worked so hard to prevent, I went up to Major Tallmadge. Such was his concentration that I stood before him a good while before he even noticed me. Then he said, "Yes, miss. Do you have something to say to me?"

"Please, sir," I began. "Is the name Robert Townsend familiar to you?"

His mouth fell open. He came to quick attention. "And if it was?"

I said, "I work for him."

It took him a moment before he said, "I beg you to explain yourself, miss."

In haste, I revealed that Mr. Townsend had placed me in General Clinton's headquarters to spy. I further told him what I had discovered. That I had been giving my information to Mr. Townsend until he disappeared. "Is he all right?" I asked.

"He's fine," said the major.

"What are you to him?" I asked.

"He reports to me," said Major Tallmadge. "Now repeat," he said with growing potheration, "what you just said, about General Arnold and this Major André."

I did as he requested. All of it. Then he said, "Stay right here." He took a step away.

"Please, sir," I called. "You must not mention my name."

Over his shoulder he said, "You haven't given it."

I watched him as he marched over to Colonel Jameson. The two began to argue hotly. Not wishing to be brought into the debate, I stayed far away so that I did not hear their words.

Their intense argument—if that is what it was— lasted quite a while. It ended when Major Tallmadge broke away and came back to me.

"Thank you," he said to me. "We have reached a

compromise. Major André will be brought back here. But Colonel Jameson insists that General Arnold be told what has happened. As for the papers Major André had on his person, they have already been sent to General Washington. I didn't inform the colonel about you. Mr. Townsend's name remains a secret."

Such was my shock, I just stood there, unable to speak. From my point of view, it was the worst possible outcome: Arnold's plan to take West Point not yet fully revealed even as Arnold was being informed his own treason had been discovered.

Major Tallmadge must have sensed my upset, for he said, "You seem to be troubled by my actions, miss."

When I found myself unable to explain, he went on, "Though you may have never heard the name, miss, I had a dear friend whose name was Nathan Hale. Years ago the British caught him. They hung him as a spy. I've waited years to have my revenge. Betrayal is a horrifying thing."

Nothing he said could have given me more pain. Still, that was also the moment that gave me a new resolve. I must speak to John André.

69

ANDRÉ WAS TAKEN to the town of South Salem and was held prisoner in a large farmhouse. A heavy guard was set about. Though I tried to find a way to him, he was not allowed any visitors.

As for General Arnold, it was just as I predicted. He was at his headquarters near West Point, waiting for Washington to arrive, when he received Colonel Jameson's letter explaining all that had happened. Realizing his plot had been exposed, Arnold abandoned his young wife and galloped to Hudson's River. Once there, he commanded boatmen to row to the *Vulture*, which was still waiting for André farther down the river. The ship, though slightly damaged, was able to take Arnold to New York. Subsequently, he put on a British uniform and fought against his countrymen.

As for General Washington, when he learned all that happened, he put West Point on alert and directed a feverish effort to strengthen the fort in case it came under attack.

In other words, because of what I did, West Point

was saved, but now John André was a prisoner, held as a spy.

And I knew only too well how the military treated spies.

Major André, guarded by two hundred mounted Continental soldiers, was taken north to Arnold's headquarters, from which place the traitorous general had fled. Once there, Major André wrote two letters. The first was to General Clinton, explaining what had happened, blaming himself and no other for his capture. He had not followed Clinton's orders to remain in his British uniform, had passed into American lines, and carried incriminating papers.

The second letter was to General Washington. In this letter, he admitted he was a British officer but insisted that he was not a spy, that he had been acting under the protection of General Arnold.

Washington made no reply, save that André was taken west across the river, first to West Point, then south, to the village of Tappan. In all his movements, he was accompanied by many troops. Major Tallmadge was at his side.

I too went along.

After André came back to South Salem, once again John Paulding asked me where I wished to go.

"I need to see what happens to John André," I told him.

He did not ask the reason. Though I believe he sensed

my unease, I did not share my troubled thoughts. In truth, I am not sure I could have expressed them. I hardly understood them myself. I only knew I must speak to André. Had I not caused this history to happen? I must see it to its end—whatever it might be.

Mr. Paulding borrowed a horse and bade me ride behind him. Thus it was that we went on to Tappan, following after André. In all this time, just as Mr. Paulding had promised, he treated me as if he was my brother.

News of André's capture and Arnold's treason spread everywhere. The whole countryside was in a state of much unsettlement. One might say it fairly seethed. Soldiers were everywhere. Many citizens came to Tappan to watch, exchange gossip, or to gain a glimpse of André.

Washington ordered that André be put on military trial for being a spy. It was quickly done. Major John André was found guilty.

He was condemned to death by hanging.

Something else happened. Whereas Arnold's treachery was widely known and hated, André became a figure of sympathetic fascination. I believe it was because, surrounded by our regular army, with men of high rank, he regained his dignity. He did more, keeping himself in as distinguished and dashing a manner as he ever did. Though he was imprisoned and guarded in a house, he was fed and cared for with the care and consideration due his rank and his person and because he was seen as a gentleman. How different an imprisonment as compared to the sugarhouse and the *Good Intent*.

What was my reaction to all of this? No person was ever sicker of heart.

Ah, but what did I *do*?

Though André was under a sentence of a hanging death, attempts were made by General Washington to exchange André for Arnold, who was now with General Clinton in New York City. The exchange did not happen. But André's servant, Peter Laune, arrived in Tappan, I know not how. When he came, he brought André's best and brightest uniform.

I stayed about the house where André was kept and simply crept in, taking on the role of a house servant, since I knew how well to play it. It was exactly as Mr. Townsend had once said to me, "The world being what it is, Miss Calderwood, your being a girl shall mask your true occupation."

On the very morning of Major André's execution, I gained entry into his prison room merely because I carried a pitcher of cool water.

When I entered the room, André, dressed in his elegant regimental uniform, was calmly sitting at a table, sketching. His disconsolate servant was standing at the far side of the room.

When I approached him, Major André barely lifted his eyes from his work. All he said was "Thank you, miss. You may set it down."

I did as he asked, but remained standing in place and just observed him. He was as handsome as ever. Nothing about his manner, his movements, suggested his grim circumstance. I forced myself to remember the first time I saw him. That was when, laughingly, he struck a lagging prisoner with his sword. In addition, I recalled his words when I had seen my brother on the street:

"These men have rebelled against their lawful government. They must pay the penalty for their stupidity. By the laws of all countries, rebels taken in arms forfeit their lives. They will be treated no better than they deserve. They should all be hung."

At length he looked up at me. He said, "Yes, miss. Is there something I can do for you?"

Barely speaking above a whisper, I said, "You do not know me, do you?"

He gazed at me. "You seem somewhat familiar. But I fear I cannot place you."

I just stood there.

"Ah!" he suddenly said, his face flushed with excitement. "You worked at General Clinton's headquarters. You cleaned my office."

"I did," I said.

He jumped to his feet. "Have you come to help me?"

"I was more than a house cleaner."

"I don't understand."

"I am Sophia Calderwood. When you first came to the city, you lived in our house."

He said nothing. Just stood there. But there was, I think, gradual recognition.

"Do you recall," I went on, "that when my brother

was taken prisoner by your army, I asked for your help to save him. You pledged to give it. But then, do you know what you said?"

He remained mute.

"You told me your honor as a British officer forbade you from helping him. And then you said, 'Miss Calderwood, can I in turn remind you of your age, which, I believe, is merely twelve. A promise to a girl is *not* a pledge to a lady. You are not yet a lady.' That's what you said."

Though I was finding it difficult to speak, I said, "Major André, I wanted—" I struggled to find my voice. "I wanted you to know," I went on, "you need to know that I am the one who uncovered your plot. It's I who exposed it and put an end to it."

"Then you were a spy," he said slowly. "Like they have accused—" He stopped speaking.

"You to be," I said, saying what would he would not say. "When you refused to help my brother, William, he died a prisoner in one of your loathsome prison ships. That's when I too made a pledge. I pledged that I would avenge his death and the death of his many companions. I came here to tell you I, for one, have kept *my* pledge."

He remained quiet, just staring at me. At last, he said, "Then, Miss Calderwood, you have become a lady."

He sat down and, without another word, picked up his pencil and began to draw a sketch of me.

How curious the mind. Upon that instant, I recalled what he had once told me, that, "My talent in sketching is showing people as they really are."

Not wanting to see how I really was, I hurried from the room.

❊ 70 ❊

I LEFT TAPPAN before John André's death. It is, as I said at the beginning, a terrible thing to see a man hang.

John André was buried in a grave near the gallows in Tappan, New York. Some years later, his remains were taken to England and were reinterred in London's Westminster Abbey. It was in a section known as the Hero's Corner.

I do not believe he was a hero, for he and his army waged a terrible war against my countrymen—including my beloved brother. How many perished in New York prisons? Shortly after the war, this notice appeared everywhere.

To all Printers of Public news-papers
Tell it to the whole World, and let
It be published in every News Paper
throughout America, Europe, Asia, and
Africa, to the everlasting disgrace and
Infamy of the British King's Commanders
At New-York, That during the late War,
it is said ELEVEN THOUSAND SIX

HUNDRED and FORTY-FOUR American
Prisoners, have suffered death by their inhuman,
Cruel, savage and barbarous usage on board
the filthy and malignant BRITISH PRISON
SHIP *called the* JERSEY, *lying at New York.*
Britons tremble lest the vengeance of Heaven
Fall on your life, for the blood of these
Unfortunate victims!
An AMERICAN

And this was just the *Jersey*. Not the *Good Intent* or other hulks. Not the sugarhouses. Not the churches used as prisons. What had my father said about the British: "Are they not our kinsmen and a civilized people?"

How deceived we were!

In 1824, some time after John André was laid to his final rest in England, I crossed the ocean and visited the abbey. Kneeling, I placed on his grave the faded blue ribbon he once gave me. For I knew two things: that I had caused his hanging death and that I adored him.

You see, I no longer wish to be at war with myself.

Dear Reader:

My story is done, but I remain your most humble servant,

Sophia Calderwood

GLOSSARY OF EIGHTEENTH-CENTURY WORDS:

affixedness
The state of being affixed; devoted attachment

bagwig
A wig fashionable in the eighteenth century, the back hair of which was enclosed in an ornamental bag

balked
Frustrated

badinage
Humorous, witty, or trifling discourse; cheerfulness, playfulness, banter

blank
As in not to listen

bosky
Somewhat the worse for drink, tipsy

brainwork
Thinking

bufflehead
A fool, blockhead, stupid fellow

candle auctions
An auction in which bids were taken for as long as a candle flame burned

common
In this sense, a room that was open to all, as contrasted with a private room, such as a bedroom

compass
Direction

credit
Belief

derangement
Disturbance of order or arrangement; displacement

emotion
An agitation of mind; an excited mental state tending to excite

gunwale
The upper edge of a ship's side; in large vessels, the uppermost plank-ing, which covers the timberheads and reaches from the quarterdeck to the forecastle on either side; in small craft, a piece of timber extending round the top side of the hull

fluster
Confuse

folly-blind
To act foolishly

forcibility
The quality of being forcible

glowflies
Fireflies

gossery
Silliness such as is attributed to the goose

glumming
That which looks glum or sullen

horse-stinger
Dragonfly

Hudson's River
The Hudson River, as it is called today, has been called Hudsons River, Hudson's River, the North River, and even on one (French) map as the Orange River. A British military map (the Ratzer Map, published in1776) references it as Hudson's River.

hugger-mugger
Concealment, secrecy; *especially* in the phrase "in hugger-mugger": insecret, secretly, clandestinely

hurly-burly
Commotion, tumult, confusion

in the fact
In the act

indelicacy
Rudeness

jabber
The act of jabbering; rapid and indistinct or unintelligible talk; gabble, chatter; gibberish (consider "jabberwocky")

jabbled
A slight, agitated movement of water or other liquid; a splashing or dash-ing in small waves or ripples

kinsmen
Relatives of the same family

laxy
Loose in texture

leveler
Someone who believes in making all people equal without social or property distinctions

linsey-woolsey
A textile material woven from a mixture of wool and flax; now a dress material of coarse inferior wool woven upon a cotton warp

mobcap
A large cap or bonnet covering much of the hair, typically of light cotton with a frilled edge, and sometimes tied under the chin with ribbon, worn by women in the eighteenth and early nineteenth centuries

muttonhead
A dull or stupid person

mumpish
Sullenly angry; depressed in spirits; sulky

nicknackery
Small, trifling

nizy
A fool or simpleton

pixie-led
Led astray by pixies; lost; bewildered, confused

plightful
Full of distress or suffering

plout
  To fall with a splash; to plunge or splash in water

potheration
  Confusion, turmoil, trouble

puddy
  Short, thickset; stumpy, podgy

puzzledom
  The state of being puzzled; perplexity, bewilderment

randy
  Having a rude, aggressive manner; loudmouthed and coarsely spoken

rantum-scantum
  Disorderly

resparkle
  To sparkle

richitic
  Suggesting wealth, riches

sensation
  An exciting experience; a strong emotion

shay-brained
  Foolish, silly

shilly-shally
  To vacillate, be irresolute or undecided

shingle
  Small roundish stones; loose, water-worn pebbles such as are found collected upon the seashore

stimulative
  Something having a stimulating quality; a motive inciting to action; a stimulus, incentive

swinking
  To labor, toil, work hard; to exert oneself

smutty
  Soiled with, full of, and/or characterized by smut; dirty; blackened

stuck pig
  Stupid

to rise at a feather
  To become easily upset

topsy-turvy
  In complete confusion

unknow
  To cease to know, to forget (what one has known)

unwarp
  To uncoil, straighten out

upstirring
  Stimulating, rousing

vexed
  To be annoyed

wondersome
  Wonderful

AUTHOR'S NOTE

Sophia's War contains three story threads, two of them as historically accurate as I could write them. The third, and major, thread is my invention.

The first of these stories has to do with the treatment of American prisoners by the British in New York City during the Revolution. While I had known about the notorious prison hulks in Brooklyn's Wallabout Bay, it was Edwin G. Burrows's brilliant *Forgotten Patriots* that provided me with the full depth of misery American prisoners experienced. While Burrows has estimated that some seven thousand died upon the field of battle, he provides good evidence to show that as many as eighteen thousand died in Britain's New York prisons!

Burrows's book and bibliographic sources (bibliographies being the amateur historian's mother lode) offered the kind of detail I have been able to present here. For example, even the name—however ironic—of the prison ship the *Good Intent* is real.

The other true story is that of British Major John André and General Benedict Arnold. Arnold is America's most notorious traitor and his story is an event about which much has been researched and written. For example, all the secret letters that passed between Arnold and André may be read in Carl Van Doren's *Secret History of the American Revolution.* I have quoted only a very few of them, but what is here is accurate. Indeed, the depth of research about this affair is so rich, so detailed, that I can write with confidence (for example) that the

Cahoon brothers, who rowed André to shore, muffled their oars in sheepskin, that the major gave a sixpence to the boy who directed him to Tarrytown, and that the phases of the moon in the night sky are as they were.

With all the research focused on the André/Arnold story, there are two moments that must be accorded as remarkable coincidences. The first is the driving away of the *Vulture*, and the second is the presence of John Paulding and his friends near Tarrytown, which allowed the capture of André.

By my reading, there is no convincing evidence as to how and why those things happened. It is here my fiction takes over. Sophia Calderwood is a complete invention, and it is she who links the treatment of prisoners to the capture of André. This tale is Sophia's story, or, as Ralph Waldo Emerson once said, "There is properly no history, only biography." Sophia is as true an individual as I could hope to create, and her actions provide an explanation as to what really happened in 1780.

Let it be clear, however, that beyond Sophia and her family, every character in this book is real, be it John André, Robert Townsend, Peter Laune, Dr. Dastuge, or Provost Cunningham.

History provides endlessly amazing stories. Historical fiction, I believe, can illuminate those stories with the ordinary people who make extraordinary history. Or let me put it this way: Truth may be stranger than fiction, but fiction makes truth a friend, not a stranger.

Avi

BIBLIOGRAPHY

Barck, Oscar. *New York City During the War for Independence: With Special Reference to the Period of British Occupation.* New York: Columbia University Press, 1931.

Bliven, Bruce, Jr. *Under the Guns: New York: 1775–1776.* New York: Harper & Row, 1972.

Burrows, Edwin G. *Forgotten Patriots: The Untold Story of American Prisoners during the Revolutionary War.* New York: Basic Books, 2008.

Campbell, Charles. *The Intolerable Hulks: British Shipboard Confinement, 1776–1857.* Tucson, AZ: Fenestra Books, 2001.

Decker, Peter. *Ten Days of Infamy: An Illustrated Memoir of the Arnold-André Conspiracy.* New York: Arno Press, 1969.

Ford, Corey. *A Peculiar Service: A Narrative of Espionage in and around New York during the American Revolution.* Boston: Little Brown, 1965.

Hatch, Robert McConnell. *Major John André: A Gallant in Spy's Clothing.* Boston: Houghton Mifflin, 1986.

Nagy, John A. *Invisible Ink: Spycraft of the American Revolution.* Yardley, PA: Westholme, 2010.

Rose, Alexander. *Washington's Spies: The Story of America's First Spy Ring.* New York: Bantam Books, 2007.

Sheinkin, Steve. *The Notorious Benedict Arnold: A True Story of Adventure, Heroism, & Treachery.* New York: Roaring Brook Press, 2010.

Van Doren, Carl. *Secret History of the American Revolution: An Account of the Conspiracies of Benedict Arnold and Numerous Others, Drawn from the Secret Service Papers of the British Headquarters in North America, Now for the First Time Examined and Made Public.* New York: Viking Press, 1941.

Werner, Emmy E. *In Pursuit of Liberty: Coming of Age in the American Revolution.* Washington D.C.: Potomac Books, 2009.

A Reading Group Guide for

Sophia's War: A Tale of the Revolution

By Avi

About the Book

IN 1776, the American Revolution comes to New York City and to twelve-year-old Sophia Calderwood's family. William, her older soldier brother, has been missing since the defeat of George Washington's army at the Battle of Brooklyn.

When the British occupy the city, Lieutenant John André of the British Army is boarded at the Calderwood home. He and Sophia develop a flirtatious friendship, which is tested when the girl discovers that William is being held in the sugarhouse, a notorious British prison. She hopes André can help. When he chooses not to, Sophia struggles to save her brother herself.

Three years later, Sophia becomes a spy in the headquarters of the British Army. There she finds André, now a major, working to enable a highly placed American general to become a traitor, a defection that will endanger the whole American war effort. Deciding to stop the treason—and motivated by personal revenge—Sophia becomes desperate. However, as Sophia learns, *desperation*'s other name is *deception*.

Indeed, the desperate characters in this thrilling tale of spies and counterspies act out many acts of deception, not least Sophia herself. Based on true tales of the American Revolution and carefully researched, this story will shock and enthrall even those who think they know what happened during the Revolution. *Sophia's War* is a haunting historical thriller.

The Three Story Threads

Avi has identified three "story threads" in *Sophia's War*:

Thread one is Part One: The treatment of American prisoners by the British in New York City during the Revolution.

Thread two is Part Two: The true story of British Major John André and General Benedict Arnold.

Thread three is Sophia Calderwood's story: a tale of fiction and the link between these first two threads.

Part One: Text-Generated Questions

1. When the story opens on September 22, 1776, Sophia is a surprise witness to a hanging. Explain Sophia's situation and that of her

family. How does the hanging affect her?

2. What kind of man was young William Calderwood? What influence did he have on Sophia during his life?

3. In Chapter 4, Sophia's mother snaps, "Child! What we think and what we say can no longer be the same!" What has sparked this statement? Was Sophia's father right to sign the Oath of Allegiance to King George? Find another example of how "The war made deception our way of life." (Chapter 15)

4. How does the boarder John André compare to Lieutenant André? How did his presence affect Sophia and her family? Does she feel affection for him?

5. What dangers does Sophia face as she searches for William at King's College, then the sugarhouse, and finally the *Good Intent*? What does her search show about her character?

6. How does Sophia describe the conditions in the sugarhouse? (Chapter 24) Who is responsible for these conditions?

7. Why would the British move American prisoners to a ship in the harbor and use it as their prison? In Chapter 27 Sophia says as she boards the *Good Intent* that "This was not mere disregard and ignorance. This, by multiple degrees, was murder." Explain her meaning.

8. Who is responsible for William's death? How does William's death change Sophia? Would this

same change have happened if he had died in battle?

9. The ship named the *Good Intent* is an example of irony in this story. Irony is an incongruity between what actually happens and what might be expected to happen. Explain the irony in the ship's name.

10. What do we learn about Benedict Arnold in Part One?

Part Two: Text-Generated Questions

1. "To lose a loved one is but part of living life, whereas to have a loved one vanish is a living death." How does this apply to Sophia and her family? When Chapter 29 begins, how is the family changed by William's death? How has the war changed by 1780?

2. What part does Robert Townsend play in this story?

3. How has Major John André changed since he was last with Sophia, in Part One? How could his new position affect Sophia? How did the poem he wrote for Sophia lead to his undoing?

4. Explain the importance of each of these in *Sophia's War*:

> Culper
> HESH
> Reverend Odell
> West Point
> Major Tallmadge

Anderson
Mr. Moore
Molly Saville

5. What would Sophia say was the key to her reaching the meeting place for André and Arnold?
6. How was the *Vulture* being fired upon and towed downriver a turning point in the meeting between André and Arnold?
7. What stands in the way of any adults believing Sophia and her story of Arnold's treason?
8. How does Mr. Paulding play a key role in the arrest of Major André? Why did Colonel Jameson send André to General Arnold? What motivates Major Tallmadge to intervene? How does Arnold incriminate himself?
9. Why does Sophia need to see André? What did Sophia accomplish in talking to him? How does his treatment as a prisoner differ from that which William received in the sugarhouse?
10. Should André have been hung?

Beyond the Text

1. In Chapter 2, Sophia mentions "the crimes the British had committed—the ones cited in our Independence Declaration." Read the Declaration of Independence (ushistory.org/declaration/document/). Key in on the list of grievances listed against King George III. Which of these grievances appear in Sophia's story? How did each affect the people and the war?

2. Find an instance in Avi's writing of how his attention to detail and his research adds to our knowledge of the time and place.

3. In Chapter 16, Mr. Paine is quoted: "Our new nation is a blank sheet for us to write upon." How does Sophia step out of her life to create her mark on this "blank sheet"?

4. In Chapter 2, William tells Sophia, "liberty shall always triumph over tyranny." Was this quote proved or disproved in *Sophia's War*?

5. Research the following names mentioned in *Sophia's War* and their importance in these times.

> Nathan Hale
> Thomas Paine, *Common Sense*
> John Locke, *A Letter Concerning Toleration*
> Alexander Hamilton
> King George III and his Parliament
> Loyalists vs. Patriots
> Hessian troops
> General George Washington

6. André tells Sophia in Chapter 22, "A promise to a girl is *not* a pledge to a lady. You are not yet a lady." Explain how André recognizes Sophia as a lady in Part Two.

7. *Deception* was the original title for this book. List all the ways deception was part of this story.

8. In Chapter 59, Sophia writes, "War makes

prisoners of everyone." What do you think she meant?

9. In what ways does telling the truth about herself embarrass and pain Sophia? Sophia says at the end of the story, "I no longer wish to be at war with myself." What does she mean?

10. Return to Sophia's "Dear Reader" letter at the beginning of the story. Was Sophia right to act in such a way? What did she contribute to the times? Write Sophia a letter in which you answer her.

Guide written by Jan McDonald of Rocky Mountain Readers

This guide has been provided by Simon & Schuster for classroom, library, and reading group use. It may be reproduced in its entirety or excerpted for these purposes. This guide was written to align with the Common Core State Standards (corestandards.org).

Read on for a look at another thrilling adventure from
Newbery Medal–winner Avi!

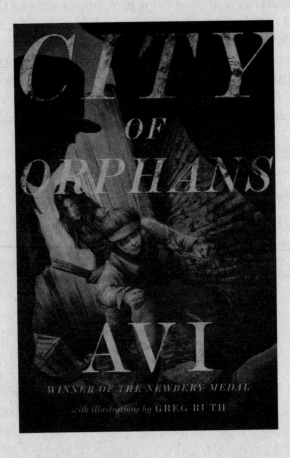

Amazing things happen.

Look at someone on the street and you might never see that person again—*ever*. Then you bump into a stranger and your whole life changes—*forever*. See what I'm saying? It's all 'bout them words: "luck," "chance," "coincidence," "accident," "quirk," "miracle," plus a lot of words I'm guessing I don't even know.

But the thing is, I got a story that could use *all* them words. 'Bout a kid by the name of Maks Geless. That's Maks, with a *k*. M-a-k-s.

Now, this Maks, he's regular height for a thirteen-year-old, ruddy-faced, shaggy brown hair, always wearing a cloth cap, canvas jacket, and trousers, plus decent boots. He's a newsboy—what they call a "newsie." So he's holding up a copy of the New York City newspaper *The World*, and he's shouting, "Extra! Extra! Read all 'bout it! 'Murder at the Waldorf. Terrible Struggle with a Crazy Man! Two Men

Killed!' Read it in *The World*! The world's greatest news-paper. Just two cents!"

Now, not everything gets into the papers, right? But see, the only one who knows what really happened up at the Waldorf is . . . Maks.

You're thinking, how could this kid—this newsie—know?

I'll tell you.

This story starts on Monday, October 9, 1893. That's five days *before* the day of that headline you just heard. It's early evening, the night getting nippy. Electric streetlamps just starting to glow. In other words, the long workday is winking.

Not for Maks. He's still on his regular corner, Hester Street and the Bowery. Been peddling *The World* for *five* hours and has sold thirty-nine papers. Sell one more and he'll have bailed his whole bundle. Do that and he'll have eighty cents in his pocket.

Now listen hard, 'cause this is important.

In 1893 newsies buy their papers and *then* sell 'em. So next day's bundle is gonna cost Maks seventy-two cents. *Then* he sells 'em for two cents each. Means, for his five hours' work, he'll earn a whole eight cents. Not much, you say? Hey, these days, six cents buys you a can of pork and beans, enough eats for a day, which is more than some people gets.

You're probably thinking, eight pennies—that ain't hardly worth working all them hours. But this is 1893. These are hard times. Factories closing. Workers laid off. Not many jobs. Housing not easy to find. Fact, people are calling these days the "Great Panic of 1893." And the thing is, Maks's family's rent is due *this* week. Fifteen bucks! For them, that's huge.

All I'm saying is, Maks's family needs him to earn his share, which is—you guessed it—eight cents a day.

Now, most days when Maks finishes selling his papers, he likes staying in the neighborhood to see how his newsie pals have done. Don't forget, this is New York City. The Lower East Side. Something always happening.

This night all Maks wants to do is to get home and eat. No surprise; he's hungry twenty-five hours a day, eight days a week. And last time he ate was breakfast—a roll and a bowl of coffee-milk.

So Maks holds up his last newspaper and gives it his best bark: "Extra! Extra! Read all 'bout it! 'Joe Gorker, Political Boss, Accused of Stealing Millions from City! Trial Date Set! Others Arrested!' Read it in *The World*! World's greatest newspaper. Just two cents! Only two cents!"

Sure, sometimes crying headlines, Maks gets to head doodling that someday *he'll* be in the paper for doing something great, like maybe making a flying machine. So *The World* would pop *his* picture on its first page, like this here mug Joe Gorker. Then Maks reminds himself that his job is selling the news, not being it. Besides, *The World* is always laying down lines 'bout Joe Gorker, screaming that the guy is a grifter-grafter so crooked that he could pass for a pretzel.

Anyway, Maks's shout works 'cause next moment, a fancy gent—top hat, handlebar mustache, starched white collar, what some people call a "swell stiff"—wags a finger at him.

Maks runs over.

The guy shows a nickel. "Got change, kid?"

"Sorry, sir. No, sir."

I know: Maks may be my hero, but he ain't no saint. Like I told you, for him, pennies are big. Needs all he can get.

"Fine," says the swell. "Keep the change."

"Thank you, sir!" Maks says as he slings his last sheet to this guy.

The guy walks off, reading the headlines.

Maks, telling himself his day is done, pops the nickel

into his pocket. Except no sooner does he do that than who does he see?

He sees Bruno.

This Bruno is one serious nasty fella. Taller than Maks by a head, his face is sprinkled with peach fuzz, greasy red hair flopping over his eyes, one of which is squinty, and on his head he's got a tipped-back brown derby, which makes his ears stick out like cute cauliflowers.

But the thing is, Bruno may be only seventeen years old, but he's head of the Plug Ugly Gang. Lately, Bruno and his gang have been slamming *World* newsies, beating 'em up, stealing their money, burning their papers.

So Maks knows if Bruno is giving him the eye, things gonna be bad. And it's not just 'bout being robbed. If Maks loses his money, he ain't gonna be able to buy papers for next day. No papers, no *more* money *and* the family rent don't get paid. In other words, no choice. Maks has to get home with his money.

Trouble is, his home is a three-room tenement flat over to Birmingham Street, near the East River. That's fifteen big blocks away, which, right now, feels as far as the North Pole.

In other words, if Maks wants to keep his money, he's gonna have to either outrun that Plug Ugly or fight him.

Don't know 'bout you, but Maks would rather run.

Maks looks over his shoulder. There's another Plug Ugly down the street. Next moment, he sees a *third*. Then *three* more. Six Plug Uglies in all, including Bruno.

Maks looks for help. He ain't exactly alone. People like to say the Lower East Side is the busiest place in the whole world. Crowds of people buying, bargaining, begging, strolling. Kids, grown-ups, dogs scrambling for dropped food. Oh, sure, some stealing. These days, folks are really hungry.

Sidewalks packed with hundreds of curb-stalls, two-wheel handcarts, plus backpack peddlers selling anything and everything, whatever jim-jam a person should want, might want, could want, can want. Food, clothing, or furniture. On the Lower East Side you can buy bent spoons, used books, four-fingered gloves, one-eyed eyeglasses, or a shoe for your best left foot. Hey, one old beard is selling cracked eggs.

Sellers crying out their goods in English, German, Italian, Yiddish, Chinese, Spanish, Hebrew, Romanian, plus so many other languages, it's like the cheapest boardinghouse in Babel.

Even the air is crowded. Crisscrossing telephone lines make the smoky sky look like ruled paper. Hundreds of signs posted here, there, everywhere. It's like someone plucked a newspaper clean of words, then stuck 'em all on walls, windows, doors, and sandwich boards, telling people to *buy, buy, and buy some more.*

Overhead, the clattering elevated steam train—called the "El"—rains down smoke, sparks, hot ash. Every time a train rackety-racks by, Maks wishes he could ride one. Trouble is, costs a nickel to ride the El. That's five cents Maks's family can't spare. If Maks wants to go somewhere, he walks.

And the neighborhood stinks too. Stinks of rotten food, sweat, smoke, plus horse dung piles. Don't forget, this is before motor cars.

So streets are clogged wheel to wheel with wagons, trolleys (bells ting-a-linging), cabs, and carts. All hauled by horses. During rush hour, if you don't look out, you're gonna be mashed or rolled out dead by metal-rimmed wheels or iron horseshoes. Maks knows kids who've been hurt, killed even. Hey, cabbies and teamsters don't care.

Neither do Bruno and his Plug Uglies.

You're asking: How come Maks don't cry for a cop? 'Cause coppers don't like newsies. Call 'em "street rats," "guttersnipes." Besides, these times, city police are hardly better than crooks. Fact, lots of those cops *are* crooks, ready to be bribed if you have the clink. Don't forget: This is before Commissioner Teddy Roosevelt started bending things straight.

Anyway, Maks ain't supposed to call for help. Kids' doings—good or bad—are just for kids. Keep that in mind.

Not that it matters. 'Cause right now, when Maks looks around, ain't a cop in sight.

In other words, Maks is gonna have to get home on his own.